A Journey
to *freedom*

A Novel By

Georgina Sinclair Caponera

Georgina Sinclair Caponera

Tate Publishing, LLC

Published in the United States of America
by Tate Publishing, LLC
127 East Trade Center Terrace
Mustang, OK 73064
(888) 361–9473

This novel is a work of fiction. Names, descriptions, entities
and incidents included in the story are products of the author's
imagination. Any resemblance to actual persons, events and
entities is entirely coincidental.

ISBN: 1-5988642-3-8

ACKNOWLEDGMENTS

Without the encouragement of my husband Joseph, I probably would never have written this book. Because of my interest in writing, he encouraged me to take college classes on the subject. I took classes at San Jose City College, San Jose State College, and at West Valley College. I loved every one of them and my interest in writing became a passion for writing. Like the heroine in the story, my life was changed by someone's words of encouragement.

I wish to thank my sister, Helen McVey of Glasgow, Scotland, who reads two to three books a week, for her hours of reading my manuscript and her very much-appreciated feedback.

I wish to thank my niece Michelle Smith, who is a first grade teacher in Antioch, California for her expertise and endless scrutiny of my grammar and her invaluable feedback.

CHAPTER 1

The sign said *Leaving Marshall County.* "Goodbye Marshallville. Austin here I come," Sarah Kincaid yelled happily as she drove her blue two-year-old convertible Mustang, letting the wind blow her hair around freely on this warm Texas day. She had never felt so ecstatic. This was the first time in her life she felt liberated, free to be herself. She was happy to be leaving her old life behind. She knew she would miss her folks, especially her dad, but she wasn't going too far away and the idea of going to college and becoming an engineer really excited her. It was her heart's desire. As a child, she never thought this would have happened to her. Sarah loved her mother, Olivia Kincaid, but wished she had never gotten involved with Church of the Chosen People. It was a cultic-type church with teachings that were different from orthodox churches. Women were second-class citizens and were taught to look as plain as possible so as not to seduce men into committing a sin. Sarah was made to dress in an antiquated style, making sure that as much of her skin as possible was covered. She also had to wear her hair long and tied back. She thought of the insults and rejection from the kids in school, but she also remembered Tyler. He was so nice to her.

She was sitting alone on a bench at school during recess. She was eight-years-old. Her dark blonde hair was in pigtails and her dress was long and old-fashioned.

"Hey Sarah!" one of the boys yelled. "Is that your grandmother's dress?"

"Hey guys, look at the shoes," another boy shouted. "They look like they belong to Laura Ingalls from 'Little House on the Prairie.'"

The boys laughed and the girls nearby all snickered. Sarah felt her face burn. She wanted to cry but she would not give them the pleasure. She hated the way she looked but it didn't make it okay for them to be so mean to her.

"Leave her alone," she heard a voice say. It was Tyler MacAulay, her big cousin Kevin's friend. He sat down next to her and smiled a very kind, gentle smile. Tyler was about twelve-years-old.

"Don't you worry, Sarah. Those girls are just jealous because you're so pretty," he told her.

She thought her heart would melt. Those were the nicest words she had ever heard. Even though she didn't believe he actually meant it, it was nice to hear him say it. She felt her little heart pumping so fast. She looked over and the boys were all leaving. They didn't want to deal with this big boy. The girls were staring at them. *They're probably wondering why this handsome senior of their elementary school would take the time to bother with Sarah Kincaid,* she thought to herself.

"One day, Sarah when you are old enough, you will make your own decisions. You can dress the way you like and wear your hair the way you like," he said, teasingly tugging at her pigtails. "And you will completely outshine everyone of them."

No one had ever given her that much attention and at that moment she knew that Tyler was the boy she wanted to marry when she grew up. All she could do was to stare up at his handsome face. She was sure she looked like a stupid little girl.

Tyler MacAulay had no idea of the impact he had made on Sarah's life. He just felt sorry for her and she was after all, his best friend's little cousin. He moved to middle school shortly after that and by the time Sarah went to middle school, he was in high school, so it wasn't very often that he came and sat with her, but that time was important to Sarah.

Sarah's father, John Kincaid, was a tall handsome man who owned a successful kitchen restoration company on the same street as the Fire Department and Sheriff's Office. His work was well advertised by word of mouth from very satisfied clients. He had many customers who came from Austin. He had restored the kitchen at home for his wife Olivia since the one thing she was interested in besides her church was cooking and she loved to clean and decorate her home. Making a comfortable home for them was her way of showing love to her husband and daughter. John was naturally a loving, caring man but due to his wife's convictions, he was restricted from showing physical love to their daughter. Olivia thought hugging and kissing Sarah on the cheek was inappropriate behavior for him. He tried to show her love in other ways, like taking her out for long walks or going horseback riding on Sundays. This gave them opportunity to talk and share things. He was not happy in his marriage, but he loved his daughter and stayed in the marriage for her sake. He knew his daughter was not happy with the way her mother dressed her but there was not much he could do about it. He had talked to his wife but he always lost the argument. He didn't know much about girl's clothes, so his argument was weak. He did win the argument that Sarah could wear riding gear on those days they went horseback riding. Olivia thought that riding a horse was also inappropriate for her daughter but John stuck to his guns on that one. He had no idea how much Sarah suffered at school. He had inquired of her as to why she never asked any of her friends over to the house but she had just shrugged her shoulders and mumbled "Uh . . . I don't know." He thought Olivia probably had something to do with it, but he didn't push the matter.

The only thing she liked about school was when Tyler would come and say nice things to her, even though it was not very often. She would keep remembering his words, *"One day Sarah, when you are old enough . . ."* In her younger years she wondered what she would do when *she was old enough.* By the time she was getting ready to move to middle school, she made a decision. She was already ahead of her class in most subjects but her favorites were math and science and she loved working on the computer. She almost knew the computer inside and out. She was also nearly fluent in French. She decided to use her lonely hours to study even more and get a scholarship to the University of Texas in Austin where she would study to be an engineer and perhaps get an apprentice job at one of the electronic companies to help her financially while attending college.

She saved up her money for the next six years doing various chores like baby-sitting for people in the church; running chores for Mrs. Jones, an elderly widow who didn't like to go out much; and from her part-time job in the ice cream parlor. Mr. Shannon, the owner of the ice cream parlor, was very nice to Sarah. She confided in him her plans to go to college. He was someone that took great interest in her and next to her father, the only person she could confide in. He knew her mother would try and hinder this idea so he never mentioned it to anyone in fear that her mother would hear of it. Sarah also had told her dad of her plans to go to college one weekend while they were out riding and made him promise not to tell her mother.

"I can't lie if she should ask. I think you should tell her, Sarah. She is your mother."

Sarah said she would when she got to high school. "After all it is just my dream for now," she had said. He had taken her to the bank to open a savings account so she could put all her earned money in it so she would have something when she graduated. He also put extra money into her account each month to help her out.

Olivia Kincaid was concerned about the money Sarah was making. "What are you doing with the money you make from the various jobs that you do?" she inquired of Sarah. "Don't you think you should put a little into the home?"

"I support this family, Liv," John jumped in. "My company is doing well and I will not take from Sarah's income," John said firmly. "I want her to save so that when she graduates, she will have some money to do whatever her heart desires."

This was what Olivia was afraid of. She was uncomfortable but she knew she had no say here. John did support them very well but she didn't like the idea of her daughter having so much decision-making power for her life.

"John, I think you spoil Sarah a little too much."

"She needs someone to spoil her a little."

Olivia knew it was time to shut up. It worried her though not knowing what her daughter was planning for her future. She needed Sarah to always be in her life.

Finally the big day arrived and Sarah graduated with a scholarship to the University of Texas. Her father was at her graduation but her mother was not. Olivia Kincaid was not concerned about her daughter's education. All she wanted was for Sarah to stay in Marshallville and marry a boy from the church. Sarah had told her two years prior to her graduation that her plans were to go to college in Austin. Olivia had tried to talk her out of the idea, but John backed Sarah up. "We can't plan her future for her, Olivia. That is her choice and there certainly isn't anything wrong with a good education. Sarah is very smart and it would be a waste for her not to go."

The day after her graduation, feeling totally free, Sarah went into town and bought new clothes and had her hair cut and styled in a layered bob to her shoulders. She even went to the department store in town and had her makeup done. "I'm not used to wearing makeup, so please don't put it on heavy."

"Don't worry," the cosmetician assured her, "you don't need much."

The girl put moisturizer on her face and just enough creamy powder and blush to give her a little color. She shaped her eyebrows briefly and put some mascara on her lashes and a little gloss on her lips. "How does that look?" she asked handing Sarah a mirror. "I can put more on, but like I said, you don't need much."

For the first time in her life Sarah actually felt pretty. "It's perfect."

She felt so good walking through town. She even had a few people turn and look at her. When she got home, however, her mother was furious.

"You will not live in my house looking like a whore. Wash that Jezebel makeup off of your face at once," her mother demanded. Sarah had expected this but she was making her statement. "And those clothes . . . they are so . . . so gaudy and all that skin showing is disgraceful," her mother continued struggling for words to describe what she thought of them. Her daughter was wearing a pair of blue capris with tiny little yellow flowers on them, a yellow tank top and a short sleeved blue blouse which she wore open.

"Just a moment, Liv, this is my house also. Sarah is my daughter and she is welcome here for as long as she likes," John Kincaid insisted. "Besides, I think she looks real pretty." Now that Sarah was leaving he was becoming more intolerant of his wife and her convictions.

The arguing went on and finally Sarah said, "I am not going to be here for very long. You know I am going to be attending the University of Texas. I am moving there in a few weeks."

"I thought you had given up all that nonsense."

Sarah and Olivia hadn't discussed college after the time, two years ago, when Sarah first told her mom of her plans. Olivia secretly hoped that Sarah would lose the notion. *After all,* she thought, *Sarah doesn't know how to live on her own.*

"I have a room at Mrs. Sullivan's boarding house," Sarah continued. "She rents only to female students attending the University. I also have written to various companies for a job during college so that I can take care of myself, and I already have an interview with one of the companies."

Olivia Kincaid could not believe her daughter had this all figured out. She knew her daughter was extremely smart but she didn't know that she could be so independent. She could see her hold on Sarah loosening. Sarah was the only person that gave meaning to her life and she was terrified. Sarah had grown up and was taking her life away from her. Olivia was searching for a wild card.

"How are you going to handle men when they try to take advantage of you? The men out there are not like the ones at church. You just don't know anything about them," her mother argued.

Sarah stared at the floor for a moment then looked straight into her mother's face. "Unfortunately that's true but I know there *are* nice men out there." She turned and looked at her dad. He was beaming at her. Obviously he was very proud that she was standing her ground. "Like Daddy, Mr. Shannon, some of my teachers, and Tyler."

"And who is Tyler?" her mother inquired, still angry.

"He's a boy who was very nice to me in school and I hope to meet up with him again someday. When I was a little girl I thought I would like to grow up and marry him," Sarah smiled a little bashfully.

"Your head is full of nonsense," Olivia yelled, brushing past Sarah and John as she marched upstairs to her bedroom, slamming the door.

"Sarah," her dad finally spoke up. "I'm very proud of you and I'm so glad you are getting out of here. I haven't given you your graduation present yet. I will give it to you tomorrow," he said smiling a smug little smile that made her desperately curious to know what he had bought her and why it had to wait until the next day. She didn't want to spoil his surprise so she didn't question him.

The next day John announced to Olivia, "Sarah and I are going into town. I have a graduation gift for her." Olivia felt a little put out that he indicated the gift was from him and not both of them. She was feeling very uncomfortable. Her world was changing so rapidly. First Sarah was taking charge of her own life and moving away and now John seemed to be separating himself from her. There wasn't a thing she could do. All she wanted was for her world to stay as it was.

Sarah's heart was fluttering. She didn't know why until they pulled into Walker's Auto Dealership. Her daddy walked over to Jim Walker and shook hands. "This way," Jim told them. She tried to keep calm but when they went over to a blue mustang convertible that had a red ribbon on it and a sign that said "Congratulations Sarah. Love, Daddy." She could not control herself any longer. She let out a squeal of delight. After checking the car she flew into his arms "Oh Daddy, thank you, thank you," then she pulled back and looked up at him. "Are you sure it's okay? What about Mom? She will be angry with you."

"You are my little girl. Nobody is going to tell me I can't give you this gift. It is my gift to you. Drive it with care."

"I will," she said, still unable to control her excitement.

When they got home, Olivia was shocked to see the car. It wasn't just that he had bought her a gift but the car also was a reminder of Sarah's new freedom. Not knowing how to express her real feelings of fear of being alone, Olivia turned to John in anger. "What are you thinking? She can't even drive."

"Yes, she can. I have been giving her lessons. I will help her get her license soon."

"I don't even feel like I am in my own home anymore," she yelled as she headed upstairs to her bedroom and slammed the door. This was her practice when she needed to get away from a situation.

"Daddy, I'm sorry. I am so happy about this new step I'm taking but I hate what it is doing to you and Mom."

A sad expression came upon his face. He took Sarah by the shoulders and stared into her eyes. "Sarah, your momma and I don't agree on a lot of things. It will be just one more thing for her to be annoyed at me for. Don't be so upset with her. She has had a hard life."

"What do you mean?"

He hesitated for a moment. "Your mom was raped as a young girl by a family friend. I think she has used this church as an excuse to hide behind. I'm not sure what their teachings are but she has used the church to keep from showing either one of us affection."

He then went on to tell her that he only stayed with her mother because he loved Sarah so much and wanted to have some influence in her life.

"Poor Momma. Daddy I am so sorry. You must have been lonely all these years."

He looked away from her as though off in his own thoughts, then looked back. "Actually Sarah, I have had a lady friend for years. Her name is Kathleen. She is always there for me when I need someone to talk to." At first Sarah was surprised but then she realized that she was not the only one who had suffered from her mother's involvement in this church. She looked at her father and smiled, "We all need someone to confide in once in a while. Does Mom know about Kathleen?"

"She knows I have a friend that I have dinner with occasionally and I think she knows that it is Kathleen."

CHAPTER 2

A month after her graduation, Sarah was packed and ready to leave. It had been a very difficult month since her mother hardly spoke to her and when she did she often referred to her as Jezebel. Sarah was glad when the day came for her to leave. She was anxious to move on to her new life and independence.

"Goodbye Daddy! Thank you for always being there for me! Thank you for the car. I'll call you."

Since Olivia wasn't there her dad took the opportunity to hug Sarah. "I am sorry your momma would not come down to see you off. It isn't that she doesn't care."

"I know. I have messed up her comfort zone but I know this is what I have to do otherwise I will end up like her. I love Momma but I can't let her convictions influence my life." Waving to her dad Sarah drove off in her convertible.

Olivia Kincaid watched from her upstairs bedroom window. She knew she should have been downstairs to say goodbye to Sarah but she felt she would be giving in to what Sarah was doing. She wanted her to stay at home so badly. She was all she had on this earth. She was feeling sorry for herself, she knew, but she felt Sarah had abandoned her.

Before leaving town, Sarah decided to say goodbye to Mr. Shannon. When she walked through the doors of the ice-cream parlor all eyes were upon her. She recog-

nized most of them as her ex-schoolmates. They didn't
know who this beautiful long legged girl in tight jeans
was. Mr. Shannon knew. He got great satisfaction to see
the look on the faces of all those kids that had been so
cruel to her. The boys were drooling and the girls looked
threatened.

"Goodbye, Mr. Shannon. I'll definitely stop by and
see you whenever I come back for a visit."

"Goodbye, Sarah and good luck with the university and your new life." Everyone was still staring as she
made her way out. She turned briefly to them and sarcastically introduced herself, "Sarah Kincaid." She went out
the door leaving them stunned. It was the best moment
of her life at that point. After twelve to thirteen years of
insults and criticism, it was wonderful to see them stare
unbelievingly at her. That was all behind her. Now she
felt as free as a bird as she drove her very own car towards
the big city.

Even though Austin was only about two hours
away, she had never been there. It actually had a skyline.
She felt the excitement flow through her body as she took
in the architecture, the big stores, the theatres and antique
shops. She couldn't wait. She parked the car and got out
and walked down the street looking in the shop windows.
She was afraid to go inside. If someone came to help her,
she wouldn't know what to say. All of a sudden, Sarah
realized just how sheltered her life had been. Austin was
exciting but it was also scary to her. She wished she had
someone with her.

She checked her directions to Mrs. Sullivan's
boarding house. She knew it was close to the university so
it wasn't hard to find.

"Come on in dear," said a jovial Mrs. Sullivan with an Irish brogue so thick you could cut it with a knife. She was short and round with a red face and hair that was quite gray. "We have all been looking forward to meeting you. My but aren't you a bonnie thing." Sarah was just hoping the girls would take to her as well as Mrs. Sullivan seemed to. She was nervous about meeting the girls, since she never had friends and didn't know how to act. Many of them were in the sitting room awaiting her arrival. Mrs. Sullivan always asked them to come down and meet the new girls, when possible. Sarah was so taken aback with the little Irish woman's hospitality that she had forgotten her manners. "Oh, I'm sorry!" she said reaching out her hand "It is a pleasure to meet you Mrs. Sullivan. I'm Sarah Kincaid."

"Of course you are dear. Come make yourself at home," Mrs. Sullivan said, leading her into the sitting room.

There were about eight girls in the room and once again she was amazed by their friendliness towards her. She felt a little shy. It was very new to Sarah Kincaid to have her peers reach out to her. They actually had smiles on their faces and one by one they introduced themselves. She knew she looked stupid just standing there looking shocked as each one shook her hand.

"Hi! I'm Trish Armstrong and this is Lisa Lansing. We will be your roommates," said a pretty girl with thick brown hair and the bluest eyes Sarah had ever seen.

"We are looking forward to having you with us," said Lisa. Both girls were about the same height, which was about an inch shorter than Sarah. Lisa had brown eyes and long blonde hair. She had a beautiful smile, which made her eyes light up. After a short while of greeting everyone Trish and Lisa took Sarah up to their room.

"Trish and I just arrived here two weeks ago, so we will all be in the same graduating class," Lisa offered as they walked to the room.

"This will be your bed," said Trish.

There were three single beds and each had a small chest of drawers by the side of them. There was a closet that was just barely big enough for the three of them. "Most of the time we wear pants and T-shirts or sweaters so whatever doesn't fit in the closet can be folded up in the drawers. The closet is mostly for our dresses, which are few," Lisa said. Sarah wasn't worried too much about not having room. She didn't have too many clothes. It would be tight quarters but the rent was reasonable and Sarah knew she could handle it. Wondering how she would get along with her roommates worried her more. She didn't know how to be a girlfriend let alone a roommate.

The house boarded twelve girls, three to a room. Each room had its own bathroom. Mrs. Sullivan had a room off the living room. It was the only bedroom on the first floor. "That way I hear when everyone comes in and then I get up and make sure the door is locked. Only then can I go to sleep," she had informed Sarah.

There were not too many rules to living in the boarding house. Everyone had to be home by eleven o'clock however. If someone broke the rule they were given two more chances but three times and the person was asked to leave. It wasn't that Mrs. Sullivan was trying to be strict but she felt a responsibility to the girls. After all, some of them, like Sarah, were just out of high school. Most of them came to Mrs. Sullivan's because their parents liked the idea of having someone watch out for them and the girls didn't mind. They had their fun and between school and lots of homework they knew they needed their sleep and they felt safe having Mrs. Sullivan as their den momma.

For the first couple of nights Sarah felt awkward trying to chat with Lisa and Trish. She didn't know their music or the television shows they watched. At first they thought she was stuck up. "I think she is very shy," said Trish. "Maybe we just have to try a little harder."

"I don't know," said Lisa "She almost sounds real religious. I mean she doesn't seem to know any music or movie stars or even television shows. What do you think she did for entertainment in Marshallville?"

On the third night she decided to go downstairs and watch television with Trish and Lisa and a few of the other girls. They were watching a movie that was supposed to be a romantic comedy but in one scene a young man and woman were undressing each other. They were not even married. She was confused and a little uncomfortable when Mrs. Sullivan walked in. "Jaisus, Mary and Joseph," she said crossing herself. The girls laughed at her.

"Oh Mrs. Sullivan, it is just a movie," said Linda a twenty-year-old who seemed so relaxed about the whole thing.

"I was raised in a very strict catholic home in Dublin," she said making *"u"* in Dublin, sound more like *"oo."* We never saw anything like this when I was a girl. They would always fade out and leave it to our imagination. Now they make us all into voyeurs."

Sarah looked at Mrs. Sullivan then at Linda. She didn't know what a voyeur was. What she did know was she was going to be learning more than computer science here in Austin. After the movie the girls went back to their room.

"How did you like the movie?" Lisa asked Sarah.

"It was quite funny. I must admit though, I was just as shocked as Mrs. Sullivan to see the young couple undressing each other." She might have been naïve, but she was honest and outspoken.

"Sarah, haven't you seen any movies lately?" Trish asked. "This one was tame."

"Actually, that was the first movie I have ever seen."

"Didn't your friends invite you to go? I mean surely there was a movie theater in your town?" asked Lisa.

"I never had friends," she said bluntly waiting for their reaction.

"I can't believe that," continued Lisa.

Sarah shared her childhood with them. She told them about her mother, the church she attended, the way she had to dress and the way the kids in school treated her.

"How terrible!" said Trish "I can't imagine not having friends growing up."

"I was an awkward kid."

"I can't believe that you were an awkward kid. When you came to this house our mouths all dropped open when you walked in the sitting room door. We were in awe of you," Trish confessed.

"In awe of me?" Sarah asked.

Trish was surprised again at Sarah's response. She realized what Sarah had told them was true. Trish felt so sorry for her at that moment. "Sarah, we're your friends. We're going to have fun together."

This was so comforting to Sarah. They actually wanted to be her friends and have fun with her. They talked for quite some time. It was midnight before they turned out the lights and went to bed.

Sarah knew she was going to love living at Mrs. Sullivan's boarding house. Momma Sullivan, as the girls called her, treated all of the girls as her own. She worried about them when they were late coming home or when any of them were sick. She was like a hen brooding over her chicks. Sarah especially felt close to her because the warm relationship she had with her was so unlike the one she had with her own mother. She also was thrilled with the friends she made at the boarding house. Mrs. Sullivan seemed to be able to make them feel like one big family. To her amazement, the girls actually seemed to enjoy being with her.

They shared their childhoods with each other. Sarah continued to tell them about the miserable years in school. She talked about her family and how her father used to take her horseback riding. She even told them about Tyler and how he made her feel better about herself and encouraged her, in a way, to start taking over her future.

Lisa was from Dallas and had gone to a private school. She had lots of friends and loved the sleepovers with them. Her father was a Finance Consultant and her mother stayed home and raised her and her two younger brothers.

Trish grew up in Austin. She was an only child. Her parents had a Real Estate business so they both worked but they were flexible with their hours so it didn't affect Trish. They were always there for her. In fact she used to help in their office with filing and some other light chores.

CHAPTER 3

Today was her interview with Mr. Stephen Taylor of Carp, Inc. She was very nervous since this was the company that had answered her request and resume and told her that they were sure they would have a part-time position for her when she got to Austin. She just hoped she would pass the interview. She wished she hadn't stayed up until midnight the night before with her roommates, since she wanted to be as alert as possible.

There was a guard shack at the gate. Mr. Taylor had told her to tell the guard her name and that she had an appointment with Stephen Taylor. He also said that he would let the guard know so he would be looking for her. The guard let her through the gate then she had to meet Mr. Taylor outside the door he had told her to go to. She thought it odd that she had to meet him outside the building. When she walked towards the door he had directed her to, there was a man standing outside. As she walked up towards him he asked, "Are you Sarah?"

"Yes, I am."

"Hi, Sarah! I'm Stephen Taylor. Glad to meet you," he said reaching out his hand to her. He put his badge into the lock on the wall beside the door and the door opened. Then she realized why she was to meet him outside. It all had to do with security. Nobody could get into the buildings unless they had a badge and in order to have one you had to be an employee who had gone through the security system. Once inside they walked to the elevator and he pushed the button. "So, when does school start?" he asked.

"In a few weeks." She knew he was just trying to keep some sort of conversation going until they got to his office. They got off on the second floor. They walked past his secretary. "Please hold my calls as much as possible."

After looking over her application Stephen Taylor looked at her apologetically and said "Sarah, the position we had in mind for you is not going to be available now for another month. I am sorry but I only just found out this morning. An emergency came up for the other person that necessitated him working a little while longer."

"I can't wait that long."

Taylor was very impressed with her obvious intelligence. Her application was impressive and her cover letter was extremely well written. "I hate to lose you, but I couldn't let him down. I can check around and see if there is anything available in another department. I haven't had time to do that since I just found out about this."

He hesitated then said, "Would you mind waiting outside while I make a call?"

Sarah waited outside for approximately ten minutes before his door opened and he invited her back into his office.

"If you don't mind me being personal, I think you have the looks for modeling. The reason I bring this up is because I have a friend that has a modeling agency, and he is always looking out for a fresh face. I just called him and he is interested in seeing you."

"But I want to do engineering work."

"Oh, I am not trying to talk you out of engineering. Obviously, that's your passion. When you graduate from college come back and see me. Or if you don't feel the modeling job would be best for you, come back in a month and the job is yours. But while putting yourself through college the modeling thing would be more money with less work and give you more time to study." He handed her a card with his friend's name, Mike Carter, on it. "Mike will be able to work with your schedule."

She was disappointed. It wasn't quite what she had expected. Working with Carp, Inc. was the job she really wanted. He apologized once more as he walked her down stairs and saw her out the door. She went back to the boarding house with the intentions of calling the other companies and arranging interviews. She looked at the card Mr. Taylor had given her. He seemed to think part-time modeling would be better for her while going through school. She had figured on a grueling schedule with school, studies and a job but knew she had to do it. Maybe this would be better. The least she should do is talk to Mr. Mike Carter and see what kind of schedule he could set up for her, if he even gave her a job. "What am I thinking about? Me, funny little Sarah Kincaid a model?" she said softly to herself.

CHAPTER 4

As Sarah walked through the doors of the Canto Agency she knew immediately she was not going to fit into this atmosphere. Huge, heavy glass doors led into a sort of octagonal shaped lobby with a beautiful Italian marble floor. The receptionist's desk was at an angle at the back of the room on the right side. A hallway with plush light gray carpeting led to six doors that Sarah assumed were offices. The first office had the name Mike Carter on it. She introduced herself to the receptionist who picked up the phone and dialed. "Mr. Carter, Miss Sarah Kincaid is here to see you," she said into the mouthpiece. "He will be right with you." She invited Sarah to have a seat in one of the burgundy leather chairs. After about five minutes she was invited into Mike Carter's office. He was a very pleasant looking man of about forty around the same age as she figured Mr. Taylor was. She could see how they would be friends. They had similar traits even though Mike Carter was very much more of a casual man than Stephen Taylor. Of course they had different types of jobs, which would account for the way they both dressed. Stephen Taylor probably always had to be ready for meetings over in the executive offices, so he dressed more business-like. She sat across from Mike Carter's desk.

"So you will be attending the University of Texas?"

"Yes, sir! I intend to be an engineer."

He studied her for a few moments. She was not only beautiful but she had a great look. It was a mixture of sensual and innocence. She had the most beautiful large green eyes with long lashes and her cheekbones were very prominent which gave her a fantastic possibility of looking very sensual with the right cameraman, which Canto had. Her lips were full and curved up at the corners. There was a look of innocence about her that he knew his camera-man would capture and use when he knew it was needed. He knew the camera would love her.

"I love engineering work. Besides I am not comfortable posing."

"We will teach you what you need to know. I will introduce you to Gloria. She is my top model and can teach you everything."

"Are you telling me I have the job?"

"You wouldn't be doing as much work as the other models, but the pay is very good and you would probably make as much or more than you would make working more hours at Carp."

"I just need to be able to pay for my rent and food. I am a very low maintenance person."

"Don't worry Sarah, you will do just fine here, believe me. Can you come back and spend a few hours tomorrow with Gloria?"

"Yes."

He reached out his hand to hers. "Okay Sarah, we will see you tomorrow. Please stop by at nine o'clock and ask for me."

She shook his hand and promised to be there.

"You are going to be modeling?" Trish asked ecstatically.

"Why didn't you tell us you were looking to be a model? After all what you told us about your past, we would never have thought that you would think of being a model," Lisa said dumfounded.

"It all happened so fast. I told you I didn't get the job at Carp but I felt stupid about the idea of me going on a modeling interview, that I was afraid to tell you because I was sure I wouldn't be taken seriously. Mr. Taylor at Carp is a friend of Mr. Carter at the Canto Agency and he made the call and suggested I go on the interview."

"What a break. But of course you would be taken seriously. Just look at you." Trish said.

"I can't believe we are rooming with a model," Lisa said. They were very happy for her.

"It's just me. Sarah!" she reminded them.

Gloria was a beautiful, tall black girl. Sarah thought she had the most beautiful eyes she had ever seen. They were almost black and had an exotic look to them. They quickly became friends. Gloria loved taking over the motherly role and this girl sure looked like she needed mothering. In the first two hours that Sarah spent with her, Gloria taught her a lot about having confidence in her appearance and taught her how to walk and apply makeup. They became very fast friends and Sarah found herself sharing her childhood with her. Like her room-mates, Gloria was taken aback that the other kids, especially the boys, could possibly reject this girl. When Sarah told her about Tyler, she knew she was going to do whatever she could to get them both together.

When Sarah got back to the boarding house she called her dad. "Hello!" John said into the phone.

"Hi Daddy!"

"Sarah, I've been waiting for your call. How is Mrs. Sullivan's place? Do you have interviews set up yet? I want to know everything," he asked anxiously.

"I've been so busy. Mrs. Sullivan's boarding house is terrific. I have two roommates, Lisa and Trish and we are very good friends. I also have a part-time job modeling. Can you imagine—me modeling? One of the models has taken me under her wing and we have taken a liking to each other."

"What kind of modeling, Sarah?" he inquired sounding a little concerned.

"It will be mostly magazines, like advertising and some local fashion shows. It is an upscale agency Daddy, so don't worry."

"Okay Sarah! I trust your judgment, but I am coming to see you soon and would like to check the agency out for my own peace of mind."

"Great! I'll look forward to that. Talk to you soon. Love you Daddy. Give my love to Momma."

A week before school was to begin, John Kincaid told his wife he was going to visit his daughter in Austin. "Would you like to go with me? Maybe seeing where she is living and how happy she seems to be will put your mind at ease," he said.

"No, I have some things I promised to do at the church," she said excusing herself. Actually she hadn't promised anything of the sort. She just didn't want to see Sarah happy in a completely different world from what she, Olivia, had created for her.

Mrs. Sullivan answered the doorbell. When she opened the door she was surprised to see a tall, handsome, well dressed man standing there. She just stood and stared at him. Finally he spoke up and said, "I'm here to see my daughter Sarah Kincaid."

"Of course. Come in. Sarah informed me that you were coming," she found herself stumbling for words. She knew Sarah's dad was coming but she wasn't prepared for the impressive looking man that he was. "I will call her down for you."

"Thank you, Mrs. Sullivan," he smiled.

She was feeling quite flustered. *How silly of me,* she thought.

Sarah ran into his arms. She was so happy to see him. It had only been a few weeks but when she saw him she realized how much she had missed him. She pulled herself away and apologized to Mrs. Sullivan. "I'm sorry, Mrs. Sullivan this is my dad, John Kincaid. Dad this is our den momma Mrs. Sullivan. She takes really good care of us girls."

"I am sure she does. Thank you, Mrs. Sullivan. It makes me feel good knowing that Sarah is here with you and the other girls."

Some of the girls came down and Sarah introduced them. He knew of Trish and Lisa from Sarah. "You're Sarah's roommates. I am very pleased to meet you."

"Thank you. We're very happy to have Sarah as our roommate. We have a lot of fun together," offered Trish. Sarah looked at her dad with a proud little smile. He knew she was looking for his approval because she finally was able to make friends and they all liked her. He smiled back and gave her a slight nod.

"Mrs. Sullivan, would it be okay to take my dad up to see our room?" questioned Sarah.

"That will be fine, Sarah. I just hope you all cleaned it up."

"Mrs. Sullivan, you always make us keep our rooms clean," laughed Lisa.

John looked around the room and saw all the girly things. *This is what she deserves. Friends, fun and a normal life,* he thought.

John took Sarah out to dinner that night. "Baby, I could not have asked for anything better for you right now. I have to say again, how proud I am of you that you took control of your life. Seeing you with your friends does my heart good," he said pounding his heart with his fist.

"Thank you, Daddy. I *am* really happy. Tomorrow I will take you to meet my other friends at the agency."

The next day John met Mike Carter; Mark, her makeup artist; Cathie, her hairdresser; and Paul, her photographer.

"Let me show you some of the pictures I have taken of Sarah," Paul said rather proudly. John smiled at his daughter. She was very pretty. She was dressed very casually and had absolutely no make up on. *I have never seen her look so happy,* he thought. Paul came back with some pictures and handed the first one to John. When he looked down at the picture he could not believe this absolutely beautiful young woman was his baby girl. Sarah was watching a little apprehensively not knowing how he would react to all the makeup and the posing.

"I can't believe this is my little girl. Paul, this is a beautiful picture. Do you have one that I can have?" Sarah was so touched that he wanted one of the pictures.

"Of course, you can have anyone of these." Paul handed him the rest and John looked through them stunned at every one of them. At that moment, Gloria walked in.

"Am I interrupting a meeting or something?" she said thinking that the handsome man was someone important in the business. Sarah turned and grabbed Gloria by the arm and brought her over to her father.

"Gloria, this is my dad, John Kincaid. Dad this is Gloria. She is my mentor in this business. She is teaching me everything."

Gloria reached out her hand. "I am so pleased to meet you, Mr. Kincaid. Sarah has talked affectionately of you often."

"I have heard a lot about you too, Gloria. Thank you for taking Sarah under your wing."

"She is an easy pupil." Glancing back at the pictures, John picked the first one he had seen. He loved them all but that was the one that took his breath away since it was the first one he saw. He took Sarah and Gloria out to lunch. "I don't think you should let Momma see that picture of me, Dad. She'll find a lot of fault with the makeup.

"I don't intend to show it to her but I have other people I want to show it off to," he said proudly. They had a good time. John got to know Gloria pretty well and liked her. He was completely satisfied with everything, the boarding house, the agency and all her friends.

When he got back home he reported to his wife everything, except the modeling agency. He didn't think she was ready for that yet. He just told her that Sarah had a part-time job. He knew that she wouldn't inquire any further into what kind of job. John was surprised when Olivia said, "Well, at least I'm glad she's happy and being taken care of." This was the most positive thing she had said about Sarah's new life.

CHAPTER 5

During her college years, Sarah was on three magazine covers as well as being pictured on many magazines inside and did a lot of local fashion shows. She earned more than enough to put herself through college and get her degree. She had gone back home only about a dozen times. Each time was just unbearable. Her mother would hardly talk to her and kept giving her disapproving looks. She finally stopped going back but her father occasionally would drive into Austin on a Saturday or Sunday and spend the day with her. Her mother didn't like it, but John Kincaid let his wife know that since Sarah was uncomfortable coming home, then he would go to her. "I'm not going to lose my daughter," he had told her. That remark stung Olivia, since she knew she had already lost her. She didn't know how to relate to the new Sarah.

Graduation day from the University of Texas had finally arrived. Her father had come down to be there for her, but not her mother. He took lots of pictures of Sarah with her two friends, Lisa and Trish. He also took some of her with the girls from Mrs. Sullivan's boarding house and some of Mrs. Sullivan, who attended graduation every year since she always had a girl being honored.

Her dad had made reservations for her graduation party at a very nice restaurant in Austin. He invited his brother, Andrew and his wife Joanne, their daughter Kim and three sons, Kevin, John and Drew. Kevin was living and working in New York, but was able to take some time off to come to her graduation. She let him know how much she appreciated him making a special trip just for her.

"Everyone is so proud of you Sarah. We're all so happy with what you have done, like putting yourself through college and working as a model and, I have to say . . . you look beautiful."

"Thank you Kevin," she said blushing slightly. "My dad helped me out but I wanted to do as much as I could for myself. It gave me such satisfaction to know that I could do it."

"Do you have a job lined up?" he inquired.

"Yes, I'm going to work for Carp, Incorporated, a high tech company. I've been hired as an engineer."

"That's right up your alley. What about the model-ing career?"

"That is over. I have one last shoot. I enjoyed it more than I thought I would, but engineering is my thing."

She had such a wonderful time being with family. It was not very often that they all got together like this and being that it was all in her honor made her feel extremely special. For the first time she felt like she belonged with the rest of them. She almost felt glad that her mom was not there. She may have quenched the joyous mood they were all sharing. John Kincaid paid for the whole meal. Her dad even brought the picture he got from Paul and passed it around. He didn't say who it was. He handed it to Kevin. He stared at it for some time being totally taken aback by the person looking back at him.

"Is this your new girlfriend, Uncle John?" he asked teasingly.

"No!" John replied feeling very smug.

"Really, who is it? She is beautiful."

"Look at it really close," John replied.

Kevin studied it for a few moments then with a look of amazement on his face he said, "You've got to be kidding." He passed the picture on and everyone had the same reaction.

"Daddy, you're embarrassing me. Believe me everyone, I had the best makeup person, hairdresser and the greatest photographer." They were all still very impressed no matter how hard she tried to sluff it off.

When Sarah managed to get Kevin alone she inquired about Tyler. "What is your friend Tyler up to these days?" she asked as casually as possible.

"Tyler is working for Kirkbride, Hood & McVey, a law firm in San Francisco."

"Oh, does he like living in California?" she asked.

"Actually, he misses Austin and so do I. We have been talking about trying to do something here on our own."

"Oh," was all she could think of to say, but she did keep the name of the company in her head.

A week after her graduation, Sarah was sitting before the mirror getting prepared for her last shoot. As she looked at her reflection she was still amazed at the work Mark, and Cathie had done on her. Her dark blonde hair was highlighted with light blonde streaks and was cut in a short, spiky style. Cathie had given her different styles during her time with the agency but this one was kind of perky and she liked it. Mark had shaped her eyebrows and had taught her how to accentuate her big, beautiful, green eyes. He also showed her how to accentuate her high cheekbones and full lips. Sarah Kincaid had the perfect face and the perfect body but Sarah was probably the only person that didn't know that. Even after the years of modeling Sarah still was dealing with the rejected, inferior child.

It was a bittersweet moment. She was excited about going to work for Carp, Incorporated but was already missing the people at the agency that she had gotten to know and like. They promised to keep in touch whenever they were in town. She experienced a lot since leaving Marshallville, especially fitting in to living in a big city, learning about style and appearance and many other things, but what she cherished most was her relationships with the people at Canto and the people at Mrs. Sullivan's boarding house.

"Sarah, Paul is ready to shoot."

"Thank you Cathie, I'll be right there." When Sarah walked into the room where Paul had his camera set up he noticed she looked sad.

"Hey gorgeous, why are you looking so gloomy?"

"I'm sorry Paul. I have mixed emotions about leaving. The staff here and the people at the boarding house are the only friends I've had in my life and now I am leaving them all. It is a very scary thing for me."

"You'll meet new friends at your job and you can come and see us any time."

She smiled at him and said "You're right," but in her heart she knew she probably wouldn't see much of them and eventually probably not at all. She had enjoyed working for the agency. Everyone was wonderful. The only time she was uncomfortable was when she received strange calls from a man that kept saying that his calling in life was to change her from a girl to a woman. She was sure the caller was talking of rape. Some of the other models said that they too had received similar calls in the past.

"Some weird people get an affixation on models just like they do with celebrities," Gloria had told her.

That reminded her of Ben, Paul's assistant. He was strange. He rarely talked and just kept staring at her. Paul had told her that he was harmless and to ignore him, but it was hard to ignore him when he was staring at her when she was trying to look sensual. A number of times Paul had to send him out because he made her very uncomfortable. Paul would make some excuse to send him out of the room.

"He is not quite all there, Sarah. He is a little slow, if you know what I mean, but he is harmless." She had never known anyone who was slow but after Paul explained that to her she was able to relax a little more around him.

"Sarah, can you bring yourself back from wherever you are?" Paul teased.

"Oh, I'm sorry, Paul, I was just reminiscing of how my life has changed so much since coming to Austin. I'm back now." She managed to get through the shoot and give Paul the looks that he wanted.

"Is Gloria around today? I would like to say good-bye to her. I know she's going to be traveling in the next day or two. I would like to see her before she goes."

"She has a shoot this afternoon."

"What time?"

"Around two o'clock," he replied.

She glanced at her watch. It was only noon and she had to stop by the boarding house. She couldn't wait around for two hours. She would just have to catch up with Gloria when she got back from her shoot overseas. She said goodbye to everyone who was there. She was disappointed that Gloria wasn't there even though she knew she would catch her later. Sarah picked up her bag and headed out. She put her hand on the handle of the big glass door when it flew open. She was thrown backwards but didn't fall down. Gloria stood there with her hand on her chest as though winded and said. "I'm glad you're still here. Girl, I can't let you go without taking you to lunch."

After catching her breath she smiled at Gloria, "That's so nice of you, Gloria."

Sarah enjoyed having this time with Gloria. It lifted her spirits. She was nervous about leaving this comfortable place where she had friends who cared for her. *What if I am unable to make friends at Carp* she thought? She could always call Gloria but she felt that after leaving the agency, even *their* relationship might wane.

"Gloria, can I call on you occasionally?"

"You call on me more than occasionally, you hear?"

Sarah smiled and nodded at her.

"When are you going to start your new job?" Gloria inquired. She knew how Sarah was feeling about leaving her friends at work and the house. She had gotten to know Sarah and knew how important the friendships were to her. *She is probably feeling separation anxiety and unsure of her future,* Gloria thought.

"I start in a couple of weeks."

"What's the reason for the long delay?"

"Well, this week I did go in and sign all the paper work. I went through security procedures and got my picture taken for my badge. Look at my badge. It makes me feel so important," Sarah said, showing Gloria her badge with her picture and employee number on it.

"Nice picture."

"I also want to take a little time and go see my parents. Other than that, just hang out, rest and take time to buy some business clothes. Maybe I'll come back and bug you all at the agency."

"None of us would mind that but I have a better idea," Gloria said as she sat back in her seat looking smug. "You told me Tyler was working at a law office in San Francisco. Why don't you take a little trip and touch base with him?"

"I haven't talked to my cousin Kevin since my graduation last week. I didn't have much time then to question him too much about Tyler. Maybe he has a girlfriend now or even a wife."

"You're just checking in as a friend, not a love interest."

"Gloria, I don't know if I have the courage. I haven't seen him in about ten years."

"You're in San Francisco vacationing and you happened to remember he was there. At least call him and see where it goes from there."

"I guess it can't hurt. I'll do it. In fact my friend Trish is moving there next week. Maybe I can travel with her."

After giving Gloria a hug and promising to get back to her on the San Francisco trip, she drove to the boarding house to say goodbye to Mrs. Sullivan and the girls and to pick up her bags and computer. There were some new girls being introduced. It took Sarah back to the day when she first stepped over the doorstep of Mrs. Sullivan's home. Some of the girls she had shared the home with had already left. Trish had moved back in with her parents, who lived just outside Austin, until her move to San Francisco. Lisa had accepted a job offer in Dallas and had already moved there.

"You take good care of yourself, dear and don't let them work you too hard."

"I will, Mrs. Sullivan. Could I stop by some Saturday morning and have a cup of tea with you?"

"I would love it. Just give me a call and I will make sure and bake some of them Irish scones you love so much."

"Thank you Mrs. Sullivan. Here is my phone number in case you ever want or need to call me."

"This is the hardest part for me Sarah. You can't imagine how many young girls I've had to say goodbye to and never see them again. I'm so glad you'll be coming to see me at times."

Mrs. Sullivan picked up a couple of Sarah's bags and a couple of the girls helped with the rest of her bags and her computer.

Her apartment was furnished. Besides her clothes, the only other possessions she had were her computer and books. She believed someday she would have her own home and would furnish it the way she wanted but in the meantime this suited her just fine. The only thing she needed was company like Trish, Lisa or Gloria. She suddenly felt lonely again. She called Trish.

"Hi Trish! It's Sarah."

"Hi Sarah! Are you in your new apartment yet?"

"Yes, and already I'm as lonely as *The Castaway*," she said referring to Tom Hanks' character in the movie of the same name. "I miss you and Lisa so much. I don't know what I'm going to do when you move away."

"Promise me, Sarah that we will always be in touch. In the meantime, let's get together. How about grabbing a meal?"

"I have a great idea. Why don't you come over here and I will get some takeout. What would you like, Pizza, Chinese or?" They settled on pizza.

Trish arrived at Sarah's apartment around 6:30 pm that night with some soft drinks. Sarah grabbed her and gave her a big hug. "Come in girlfriend. This was a great idea."

"This is a nice apartment," Trish said looking around. About ten minutes after she arrived the pizza was delivered.

"I'm planning on taking a trip to San Francisco. Would you like me to try and get on the same plane as you?" Sarah asked.

"Great, that's exciting. I hate traveling alone. We could share the same hotel room. I *will* be busy apartment hunting so I won't have much time to sightsee," she warned.

"That's okay. I have some plans of my own."

"Oh!"

"I'm going to try and see Tyler," Sarah said excitedly.

"You're kidding! How are you going to get in touch with him?"

"My cousin gave me the name of the firm he is working for. I'll call him and just tell him that I am in San

Francisco with a friend helping her find an apartment and thought I would call and say hi! Then I'll just see how it goes from there," she said with a little proud smile.

CHAPTER 6

Sarah was able to switch seats with another traveler so that she could sit next to Trish. "Trish, I am nervous about calling Tyler, but I don't see what harm it would do to go out to lunch with an old friend, even if he has a girlfriend or wife."

"That's right. Oh, Sarah I hope it works out for you," Trish said sincerely. "I know what Tyler means to you and what a big influence he was during those awful school years."

"Me too."

"I'm a little nervous about my move," Trish admitted.

"I was wondering about that. I hope you will enjoy living in San Francisco, Trish. I can't imagine living outside of Texas."

"I visited San Francisco when I was about ten years old when my Aunt Mary lived there. I really liked it."

"But visiting it and living there is a lot different. Of course it isn't a life sentence. You can always come back."

"That's right! If for some reason things didn't work out in San Francisco, I have my parents to lean on back in Austin."

"You have me too!" Sarah reminded her.

"You're making me feel homesick already. I will miss you and my parents."

"Don't worry, you will be back and forth. I'm sure we will see a lot of each other," Sarah said trying to make her feel more comfortable about her decision to move away.

"We definitely have to keep in touch and also with Lisa. Maybe once a year we could have our own reunion, taking turns meeting in our different cities," Trish suggested.

"It would be the only reunion I would attend. I definitely will not be going to my high school reunion."

"Gosh no. But really, let's think about you, me and Lisa."

"I'll email Lisa when I get back to Austin," Sarah offered.

Sarah waited until the next day to call Tyler since she didn't want to say she had just arrived if he asked her. She didn't want to sound desperate to see him. She looked up his company in the phone book. She was nervous. She picked up the receiver and put it back in the cradle a couple of times. Finally she took a deep breath and dialed. A woman answered the phone. "May I speak to Tyler MacAulay please?"

"I think he left the office but I will try his extension." Sarah's stomach was jittery.

"Hello!" she heard his voice. She almost had to force herself not to hang up.

"Hello . . . Tyler, this is . . . Sarah Kincaid," she stammered then promptly said, "You probably don't remember me . . ."

"Of course I do. How are you Sarah? Where are you calling from?"

"San Francisco. I came here with a girl friend. She is moving here and I have some time before starting my new job so I came along."

"Gee! I wish you had been here sooner. I'm running out the door to have lunch with someone and then to the airport to catch a plane."

"Where are you going?" she asked almost desperately then felt it was rude of her to ask.

"Back to Austin. Kevin and I are opening up our own law firm. He will be leaving New York in a few days to go back home. Sarah, I will have to call you when you get back. I'm running behind."

"I'm sorry! I won't keep you. Goodbye Tyler." She hung up the phone so quickly as though that would help Tyler get on his way faster. Trish had already left the hotel to go and meet with her new employers. She was to be given a tour of the facility and meet the other employees. Sarah almost felt like she wished she were back in Austin. "Sarah Kincaid this is ridiculous. Here you are in one of the most beautiful cities in the world and you are sulking. Get out and see this place," she scolded herself. She went downstairs and picked up some brochures of the city and guides.

It was a lovely warm sunny day as Sarah walked along Fisherman's Wharf. There were boats taking people around the Bay over to Alcatraz and the Golden Gate Bridge. The ferries were called the Red and White Fleet. It was a beautiful sight to watch the Pacific Ocean come in through the Gate to form the Bay. She spent some time just watching the activity. Besides the Red and White Fleet, there were small sailboats and motorboats, but watching the numerous seals, which seemed to be waiting for the fishermen to come in, were the most fun. They made so much noise, all barking at the same time as though trying to get the tourists to throw them a treat. Even though she was enjoying it all, she couldn't stop thinking about Tyler. She couldn't believe her timing. If only she could have come a few days ago, she could have traveled back with him. She barely got to talk to him. He didn't seem too excited to hear from her. Why should he be? It had been about ten years since she saw him. She had been about thirteen- or fourteen-years-old.

As exciting as San Francisco was, she was sad. She was so looking forward to being with Tyler. After all, he was the reason she came to San Francisco. She imagined walking along the Wharf with him by her side taking her to all the fun places this city had to offer. She still didn't know if there was a woman in his life. She was so deep in thought about him that she didn't notice a Mime walking along side of her making sad faces as though to emulate her. For a moment he made her laugh so she took a dollar from her wallet and gave it to him. There were many artists and musicians on the sidewalks displaying their art. Vendors had brought in temporary stands and tables to display their goods, which mostly consisted of touristy tee shirts and sweatshirts bearing the name *San Francisco* and a picture of a San Francisco landmark. There were also quite a few stands where the vendors were selling jewelry. This was a very lively part of San Francisco with people bustling around, street musicians playing their instruments and singing their songs with seals barking in the background. Sarah was amused at the Japanese tourists getting their pictures taken with what they assumed were the locals. They would bunch up together in such a large group that you could hardly see the "local" that agreed to have their picture taken with them. The smell of crab cooking in their big boiling pots by the outdoor seafood vendors made her realize how hungry she was.

She had walked quite a distance. It was about 12:30 pm and she knew she was going to have to eat soon. She hadn't eaten breakfast since she was hoping that maybe she and Tyler would go out to lunch together. She was at Pier 39 and decided to go into the Crab House for lunch.

Tyler was lunching with a client going over last minute papers when Sarah walked in. She was dressed in white Capri pants and a pale green cotton shirt that tied at her midriff with a darker green tee shirt underneath. Tyler couldn't take his eyes off her. He thought she looked like a goddess. He didn't know that it was Sarah of course, since he hadn't seen her since she was a young teenager and an awkward one at that. As he was leaving he made sure that he gave her a smile of approval. He wished he had more time to try to get to know who she was. Sarah noticed and appreciated this handsome man's flirtatious smile. He made her think of Tyler for some reason.

After lunch she walked back down the Wharf towards The Cannery. At the Boudin Bakery and Cafe people were sitting outside eating. One of the most popular dishes at the Bakery was clam chowder served in a sourdough bowl. The restaurant would cut off the top of a round loaf, then scoop out the bread and make a bowl out of it and pour in the soup. The top could be used to dip in the soup. This was the best sourdough bread in the world. San Francisco had the best environment for making it, Sarah learned. She spent time looking in the shops at The Cannery then walked up towards Ghiradelli Square then back to the cable car turn around. She got off at Chinatown and walked around stopping in at the shops looking for something special for her new apartment but she just couldn't focus on anything. *He said he would call me when I got back, but he didn't even ask for my phone number. He and Kevin would be getting a new number. Of course I could get Kevin's from his parents. I don't really want to contact Tyler again. I don't want to seem too eager. What would Gloria advise me to do? I'm going to have to call her and tell her what a fool I had been, coming all the way to San Francisco only to be . . . to be what? He had his plans all made before I came. It wasn't as though he had rejected me. He did have a plane to catch,* she thought. She was getting tired of walking. She called Trish and arranged to meet her at the Cathay House on Grant Street for a Chinese dinner. She went into the restaurant and made reservations for seven o'clock.

Sarah was already seated at the table when Trish came in. "So tell me?" Trish asked excited to find out what happened with Sarah's day with Tyler.

"Trish, you won't believe it. I got a hold of him, but he was in a hurry to catch a plane to, guess where?"

"Where?"

"Austin."

"Oh no! When will he be back?"

"Well, the good news is, he is not coming back. He and my cousin Kevin are starting their own practice in Austin. Well, I'm not sure if it is good or not. He didn't seem really excited to hear from me and I still don't know if he has somebody."

"Don't worry girlfriend, he will be excited when he sees you. He'll be blown away."

"I'm sorry for sounding so down Trish. I actually had a beautiful day walking around Fisherman's Wharf, The Cannery and Ghiradelli Square."

"Well, I'm glad you had a nice day, even if you didn't get to meet up with Tyler. You will soon though."

"I didn't realize until today how much I have changed. The day I arrived in Austin, I parked my car and walked up and down the street looking in shop windows. I was afraid to go inside in case someone would come to me to ask if I needed help and I wouldn't know what to say. Today, I walked around a strange city; walked into, not only stores, but also art galleries near the Ghiradelli Square and discussed artwork with the curators; ate by myself in a restaurant and took the cable car to China-town. It made me realize the confidence I've gained over these past four years. Thanks to all my friends in Austin."

"Oh, you have changed, Sarah. I think the modeling was the best move you made. It taught you a lot."

CHAPTER 7

It was good to be back home. She ended up spending almost a week in San Francisco. She helped Trish find an apartment with another woman, named Carol. She seemed really nice and she and Trish hit it off real well, which sort of made Sarah feel a little jealous. After all, Trish had been her first best friend, but she was happy for her knowing that she wouldn't be alone. She certainly knew how that felt. She promised to come back and visit another time.

It was rather late when she got home on Thursday night. The plane had been delayed and she was tired so she thought she would wait until tomorrow to make her calls.

She slept a bit later than usual. She almost forgot she had some appointments to have her hair done and a manicure and pedicure. She didn't know why she was having that done except she had become accustomed to having her hair and nails look nice. By the time she got back to the apartment it was about four o'clock and she hadn't even called her dad yet to let him know she was back home from San Francisco plus she had other calls to make. "First things first," she said to herself as she picked up the phone and dialed. "Hello Daddy, I just wanted to call you and let you know I'm back home. How is Mom doing?"

"Hello darling your mom is doing fine. She asks a lot about you. What you've been doing; where you are working; where your new apartment is. She seems to be very interested. I keep telling her to give you a call. We just have to be patient with her, but she is showing a lot more interest lately. How was your trip?"

"It was great. Trish found a nice apartment and roommate. San Francisco is a beautiful city, Daddy. I did quite a lot of walking around it." They talked for about ten minutes. "I have to make some other calls Dad, so maybe I will come and see you and Momma soon. I'll call and let you know when."

"That would be great sweetheart. I'll let your mother know you called. Goodbye."

She hung up the phone. She was anxious to get in touch with Kevin to find out if Tyler had told him that she called him in San Francisco. She next called Kevin's parents and got his phone number and address.

"Hello Kevin, this is Sarah. I heard that you were coming back so I got your number from your folks."

"Sarah, it's good to hear from you. I tried calling you yesterday but you weren't home. I got your number from your dad. I figured you might still be in San Francisco so I didn't leave a message."

"Oh, you heard I was in San Francisco? Did my dad tell you that?" she said trying to find out if Tyler had mentioned her.

"No! Tyler told me you called him. He felt bad that he didn't have time to talk with you let alone see you." She smiled to herself. So he had talked about her to Kevin. It may be a little thing, but anything positive was big to her.

"Say, we're getting together tonight for dinner. Why don't you join us?" he continued.

"Oh I don't want to intrude. Maybe Tyler wouldn't want me there. I mean maybe he just wants to be with his buddy. You know, boys night out."

"I know he wouldn't mind, but if you feel awkward about it then how about you and me for lunch on Monday?"

"That would be great." Sarah wrote down the name of the restaurant and the time they were to meet. "Okay Kevin, I'll see you on Monday."

"I'm looking forward to it. Bye Sarah."

She felt disappointed that he didn't try and talk her into meeting with them tonight. Actually she was feeling quite depressed knowing that they would be together having a good time and she would be at home alone. She hoped that Kevin would mention to Tyler that she was home.

Maybe I should give Gloria a call, she thought. Just as she reached for the phone, it rang. She picked it up, feeling excited as she thought it might be Kevin calling back to encourage her to meet with them. There was no answer to her greeting. The person on the other end did not hang up but didn't say anything either. Sarah asked who was calling, but still there was no answer. She hung up the phone and called Gloria.

"Gloria, Sarah here. How are you?"

"I am fine. I'm getting dressed to go out with, guess who?"

"Who?"

"Martin Crawford, the director."

"Gloria, how great. I'm so happy for you."

"He's interested in talking to me about a part in his new movie. But I will get back to you on that. Tell me how you did in San Francisco. Great, I hope."

Sarah told her about her San Francisco blunder and that Kevin had invited her to join him and Tyler for dinner and that she had turned him down.

"Why on earth did you do that?"

"It would be awkward for me. I don't know if Tyler would like me to be there. I mean he and Kevin had plans and it didn't include me."

"Well they didn't know you were back. Well at least you have a better chance of seeing him now that he has moved back to Austin."

She talked to Gloria for about fifteen minutes. As soon as she hung up, the phone rang again.

She was expecting to pick up the phone to listen to the silence again but instead she heard,

"Sarah, Tyler here. I'm sorry I couldn't talk to you last week but give me another chance. Come join us tonight. Please!" He waited for a response but there was none.

"Sarah, are you there?"

Her heart started racing. "Yes Tyler, I'm here." She couldn't believe her ears. He was actually pleading for her to meet with him. "I didn't think you would want me to interrupt boys night out."

"This is a reunion. I haven't seen Kevin in a few years and I haven't seen you since you were a kid. Of course we both want you to join us."

"I would love to join you. Just tell me where and when."

"The Irish Pub at seven-thirty. I'm really looking forward to seeing you, Sarah."

"I'm looking forward to seeing you too, Tyler. It will be fun to see how we have all grown up," she said laughing.

She hung up the phone and jumped up and down and did a little dance, squealing the whole time. She ran into the bedroom. It was already five o'clock and she wanted to look extra special. Now she was glad she had her hair done along with her manicure and pedicure this afternoon. Rather than taking a shower she decided to sit in the tub and bathe in some of her scented aromatherapy oil. She soaked for half an hour, going through her wardrobe in her mind. She was trying to decide whether to go casual or wear something a little more dressy or sexy. "I wonder what Gloria would do?" she said out loud then she smiled. "I know what Gloria would do. Definitely she would dress in some hot little number." She had to remember to call Gloria back and tell her about Tyler's phone call. After all, this had all been her suggestion and it was looking good.

Even though she had shaved her legs that morning she wanted to make sure they looked their best so she shaved again. Everyone at the agency commented on how great her legs looked. She even did an ad for shoes where only her legs and feet were photographed. After drying off she applied moisturizer all over. She was glad that she inherited her father's skin color. Her skin was a very light tan and in the summer it had a very healthy look to it. She took special care with her makeup then headed for the bedroom to find that sexy dress.

"I better eat a little something. Between the liquor and the butterflies in my stomach I might get sick. Oh good grief, that would be just great. Throw up in front of him," she said talking to herself nervously but also excitedly. She wanted to look her best. She walked into the kitchen and ate a leftover taco and some yogurt. "Why did I eat that taco? It had garlic in it. I better brush my teeth again."

After coming out of the bathroom she went back to her bedroom. She knew she wanted something short. If her legs were as great as everyone said then she wanted to make sure Tyler saw them. She had quite a few short dresses, just about a couple of inches above her knees. She didn't like to wear them too short. Even the new Sarah would not have that much skin showing. Her eye caught the black knit one with the little spaghetti straps and she knew that was it. She put it on and checked herself in the mirror. "I hope this is the right one." She found a pair of black sandals with three-inch heels and felt they were perfect for the dress. She hoped they didn't make her too tall. She didn't know how tall Tyler was. She put her hand on her stomach, "please calm down." Turning to look at the clock she was amazed that it was already seven o'clock. "It will take me about twenty minutes to get there but I don't want to get there first so I will leave here about seven-twenty." She picked up the phone and dialed Gloria and told her about Tyler's call.

"Do you think I'm dressed right?"

"Girl, you could dress in sweats and look great but it sounds that you have done good. I'm glad all my training has rubbed off on you."

"Thanks Gloria. I have you to thank for everything I know about fashion."

"Break a leg tonight girl," Gloria teased.

CHAPTER 8

Kevin and Tyler were already at the restaurant.

"I'm glad Sarah is going to join us tonight. I felt bad not seeing her the day she called me in San Francisco but I was late for a lunch appointment. Talking about lunch that day, I saw the most beautiful woman at the restaurant. It was a good thing I was through with the business I was doing. When she walked in, I hardly knew who I was let alone where I was and whom I was with. She completely had my attention. I was running for a plane so I had no time to pursue her."

"Too bad. But California doesn't have all the beauties; we have our share here in Texas."

"I know but I have never seen such a beautiful woman and I don't think I will see that twice."

Kevin changed the subject as he was thinking of his cousin. "I haven't seen much of Sarah since she came to Austin to attend college. I probably saw her just one or two times and then for her graduation. Mostly because both our schedules were so busy. Of course I've been in New York these past three years," he said. "But now that I'm back and she is out of school and not modeling anymore maybe I will see more of her. I hope so."

"Did you tell me she was modeling?" Tyler inquired.

"I thought I did but it . . ."

"Wait don't turn around right now," Tyler interrupted "but you have to see this woman that just walked
in. She almost looks like the woman I saw in San Francisco . . . whew!"

Kevin turned around and waved.

"What are you doing?" Tyler asked.

"I am waving Sarah over to our table," Kevin
replied.

"That's Sarah?" Tyler asked with his mouth open
while staring at Sarah unbelievingly as she walked towards
them. He couldn't decide which part of her to look at. She
was beautiful from head to toe. But the legs were so unbe-
lievable he found himself staring at them even when she
was right at their table. Sarah was still trying to calm the
butterflies in her stomach and hoped that she wouldn't say
something stupid.

She first went to Kevin and gave him a hug. "It's
great to see you again, cousin," Kevin said. "You look even
more spectacular than you did at your graduation party."
Sarah smiled knowing that she took extra special care for
this party

"It has been a long time since I have seen you,"
Sarah said turning toward Tyler. "I wasn't sure you would
even remember me," Sarah said trying to keep calm.

"Oh I remember you but I wouldn't have recognized you. Do I get a hug also? Maybe an even bigger one
since it has been so long," Tyler said grinning.

"Of course you do." *This is where I'm going to fall
apart. I hope he doesn't feel me shaking,* she thought. He
put his arms around her and gave her a huge hug. Other
than an occasional hug from her dad and Kevin, who were
family, Tyler was the only man she had come in such close

contact with. She was amazed at the hardness of his body. He had no fat or flab. He was solid. He stood back and let her move into the middle of the booth. Sarah felt so weak that she stumbled a little. Tyler grabbed her elbow, "Steady there. And you haven't even had a drink yet. Speaking of which, what *would* you like to drink, Sarah?"

"I would like a glass of sparkling water with lemon" she replied in a rather weak voice. Waving the waitress over he ordered her drink.

Lifting their glasses Sarah said, "May your business prosper and your friendship continue to bloom."

"May you do well in your new job and enjoy your new apartment," Kevin said.

"Here! Here!" said Tyler. After a while they were laughing and Sarah felt very relaxed Tyler was staring at Sarah "You *are* the girl I saw in the restaurant at Fisherman's Wharf, aren't you?" he asked.

"And you are the man that smiled at me as you walked past my table."

"So we did see one another that day and didn't know it," he said laughing.

"That's amazing. I was feeling so disappointed that I wasn't able to meet up with you, and there you were," Sarah said

Sarah felt a thrill go through her. He had sort of flirted with her in San Francisco when he didn't even know it was she. So she needn't think that he was just being nice to her now because she was Kevin's cousin. He was obviously attracted to her.

They ordered dinner. Sarah was glad, as she didn't have very much to eat that whole day. She was feeling very comfortable being with Tyler. She told the story of

GEORGINA SINCLAIR CAPONERA

the day she left for Austin and stopped by the ice-cream parlor and how she got back at all those kids that had been mean to her.

"I would love to have been there to see their faces," laughed Tyler. "I remember how mean they were to you."

"The best part though was the call from Sandy Connelly. After I had my face on a few magazines, she called me. She was the one that was most popular with the in-crowd and the one who was snobbiest to me."

"What did she want?" Tyler inquired.

"Oh! The girls were having a sort of reunion and would love for me to come." Sarah smiled impishly. "I said, 'I'm sorry who did you say you were?' She sort of hesitated then said 'Sandy Connelly from your high school class.' Then I answered and said 'Oh you know, I didn't take the time to get to know any of the kids at school. All my friends were those at the University and the models I work with. But thank you for asking me anyway. Goodbye,' then I hung up." They all laughed.

"I know it was kind of mean but I figured thirteen years of them all being mean to me, this would probably be my only chance to get back, so I couldn't resist."

"Good for you Sarah!" Kevin said. A short time after dinner Kevin announced that he had to go because of an early golf game in the morning. Tyler glanced at his watch. "Hey man, it's only ten o'clock." Kevin was already up on his feet.

"I know but I had an early start today and another tomorrow and I'm feeling beat. You guys stay and have a good time." Actually Kevin saw that things looked good between his cousin and best friend and wanted to give them some time to get to know one another without him in the loop.

"Would you care for some coffee?" Tyler offered.

"That sounds great."

They talked about that day in San Francisco when he had seen her in the restaurant. "I noticed you immediately. I even mentioned you to Kevin tonight and said I didn't think I would ever see anyone that beautiful twice and here you are, sitting talking with me. I can hardly believe it."

"Tyler MacAulay, you are just flirting with me," she said coyly wanting to hear more.

"No, I'm telling you the truth. I don't usually smile at strange women."

She finished her coffee and Tyler asked if she wanted anything else. "No! Thank you Tyler."

He didn't want the evening to end so soon. He was enjoying her company very much and she was so great to look at and comfortable to be with. She didn't put on any airs or do some of the girly things that annoyed him. *She is an engineer for goodness sake, more than she is a model. How could this beautiful woman be so technical?* But as intelligent as she was there was still the insecure little girl in her that would surface occasionally and Tyler noticed it. *What was she insecure about?* he wondered. Bringing his thoughts back to figuring out how to keep her a while longer, he blurted out "I have a horse ranch. It isn't huge but it is nice and peaceful there."

"I really love horses. My father used to take me riding occasionally on Sundays. Maybe some day you can show me your ranch."

"How about now?"

"Oh I don't know Tyler. I would still have to drive home and it is getting a little late." Sarah said a little unconvincingly. She didn't want the evening to end either. She loved being with him. This had been her dream for so long. "I think it would make more sense if I came over tomorrow," she said finally getting her senses together. "I wouldn't be able to see very much tonight and besides I'm not exactly dressed for touring a farm."

"You're right. How about coming over around ten o'clock. That way I can give you a tour of the house, then I will give you a tour of the ranch horseback style?"

"That would be great. I'm looking forward to it." Everything was turning out much better than she had hoped. He gave her directions to his home then he walked her to her car. There was an awkward moment as they were trying to figure out how to say goodnight. Finally he gave her a little hug and opened her door. "I'll see you tomorrow," he said as he closed her door.

CHAPTER 9

It was eleven o'clock by the time she got home. She decided it would be okay to call Trish since it was only nine o'clock in San Francisco. She just had to tell someone of the evening's events." Hello?" Trish said as she answered the phone.

"Trish, Sarah here. How are you?"

"I'm fine Sarah. How was your flight home? It seems like you just left here."

"Everything was fine. Trish I called to tell you about my evening. Guess who I was with?"

"Tyler? How did it happen?"

"I called Kevin and he told me he was meeting with Tyler for dinner then a short while later Tyler called and invited me to join them. I had such a great time Trish, and he has invited me over to his farm tomorrow and we are going horseback riding. I'm so excited. I think he likes me."

"He must, otherwise he wouldn't have invited you to his home. I'm really happy for you Sarah." They talked for about half-an-hour then Sarah got ready and went to bed. She set her alarm for eight o'clock to make sure she had plenty of time to bathe and look her best. In spite of her excitement she fell asleep easily and woke up feeling really refreshed.

Tyler had gotten up early as he had some prepara-tions of his own to do. After taking a shower he went to the kitchen and made some coffee. He took the chicken from the refrigerator that he had put there last night to thaw out. He prepared it for frying by rolling it in flour then in an egg wash then rolled it in breadcrumbs. While the chicken was frying he tossed a salad leaving the dressing off until it was time to eat it. He was glad he had a loaf of his favorite country bread. By the time the doorbell rang, he had everything put together for a picnic. He felt like a teenage boy in love for the first time. He wasn't quite sure what it was about Sarah, besides her beauty, that made him feel that way. He opened the door and there she was. She looked different from last night. She had no makeup on but her face looked so fresh. Her hair was tied back in a ponytail and she had on jeans and a bright green shirt that made her eyes look greener than they did the night before. She looked so outdoorsy.

"Hi!" she said with a big smile that lit up her whole face. "I brought my riding boots," she said holding them up to show him.

"Great, come on in," he said opening the door wide for her. "Please excuse the mess. I haven't quite settled down yet. There are quite a number of unpacked boxes so watch your step," he said pushing back two of the boxes. "Lucky for me, my mom had the house in order for me moving in, but I still haven't put some of my books and knick knacks away." Tyler's Golden Retriever came running to the door to greet her.

"Hey, what's your name?"

"This is Lady. She will probably come with us on our ride. She loves to run along with me every time I go out."

"Hi Lady, I'm glad you're going to come with us," Sarah said, rubbing Lady behind the ears. "My Dad has a dog. We never had one when I lived at home, but after I left my Dad bought it for Mom thinking it would keep her company. She's not an animal lover but Dad enjoys Tweed's company."

"Where did the name Tweed come from?"

"Tweed is the name of the river in Scotland where Border Collies come from."

Tyler walked her into the kitchen. "It smells wonderful. Have you been cooking?"

"I made some chicken. I thought I would take along some lunch and we can picnic at my favorite place."

"Sounds wonderful," Sarah said still not believing she was in Tyler's home. She had butterflies in her stomach. She wanted to be calm and just be herself but she kept having thoughts of doing or saying something stupid.

After touring the inside of the home Sarah turned to Tyler and said, "This home is so comfortable. I would love to live in it." *That's it,* she thought, *I knew I would say something stupid. Now he will be thinking I want to marry him.* "I mean a home like it," she said blushing.

"I know what you meant Sarah," he said laughing although thinking that he wished she did live in it *with him.* "I'm glad you feel that it's comfortable because that's exactly how I feel about it."

She hated the fact that she still sometimes blushed. It made her feel like a child. Tyler on the other hand thought it was refreshing. *She is so smart, yet so childlike,* he thought.

When Sarah looked back at him she found him staring at her. Once again, she felt her face warming up.

"I will put my boots on," she said giving her an excuse to turn from him. She walked into the living room where she had left her boots. Tyler walked in after her. "Nice looking boots," he said helping to push them on her foot.

"Daddy bought them for me when he saw how much I loved riding."

"Well you definitely are better dressed for riding than you were last night. This was a much better plan. I think I just didn't want the night to end," he said.

"I didn't either," she confessed, surprising herself.

They stood looking at each other for a brief moment then Tyler noticed that Sarah was starting to look uncomfortable.

"Okay, let's go meet the horses," he said putting his hand on her elbow and leading her out. "Come Lady."

"This is Sandy," he said introducing Sarah to the horse in the first stall.

"The name is perfect for her. Her coat does make you think of sand. She looks so elegant," she said stroking her and giving her a carrot that they had brought down from the house. "You are beautiful, Sandy."

"I think she will be the perfect horse for you to ride," Tyler suggested. Moving on to the next stall he introduced her to Mac. "This is the horse I ride the most," he said of a magnificent big chestnut colored horse. "Mac was my grandpa's nickname, so he is sort of named after him," Tyler said affectionately.

"What a beauty. He is so majestic," she said admiring Mac. "He is your horse. I can tell and I think he knows it too."

The other two horses were Jake, a large gray stallion and Maddy, a beautiful brown mare with a blonde mane. "Are you going to breed any of them?" Sarah asked.

"I'm thinking of breeding Maddy next spring but I will have to see how things are going for me as far as our law firm and my life in general," Tyler said. "I would want to have time to be a part of the process. I have a guy working for me who knows all about horses. My dad hired him when he and mom lived at the house after grandpa died. His name is Joe. You will probably meet him some day. But if I start breeding, I will have to have more help. That's why I have to see how our business is doing."

"Tyler, if you do breed Maddy, please invite me over to see the foal," Sarah said almost pleadingly.

"You bet!" he said then turning towards her he said very seriously, "I've never been with a girl who loves horses the way you do. That means a lot to me."

She felt something happen between them at that moment. It was as though they were bonding. Horses were something that was very dear to both of them. Horses were part of her childhood that she loved. It was those very special times when she was with her father and she would ride laughing with the wind blowing her long hair back. That was the only time she could let her hair down, literally. Her mother would have been horrified if she had seen her daughter like that.

Horses were part of Tyler's childhood too. He loved spending the weekends with his grandpa, listening to all his stories.

"Let's saddle up. Can you lead Sandy out? I'll get Mac," Tyler said in a soft, gentle voice. Pretty soon they were saddled and ready to ride.

"It feels wonderful to be back in the saddle," she said smiling.

"I thought you were about to break out into a song," he said smiling back at her. They trotted out to the pastures with Lady running alongside. It was a lovely day. The sky was as blue as could be. "You don't know how good I feel right now, Tyler."

"You don't know how good you *look* right now," he said admiring her sitting on top of Sandy. That surprised her and she turned to look at him and without thinking said, "Do you think so?"

"Sarah, you truly are unaware of how beautiful you look. That amazes me. How can you look in the mirror and not see that?"

"Tyler, I'm a computer geek and a nature lover. I don't think of how I look. I spent years being laughed at because of how I looked."

"Well, let me say that you are a sight for sore eyes to this cowboy," he said smiling at her.

"Thank you, Tyler. I really do appreciate you saying that," she said. Then changing the subject she said, "On the way back to your house, could we gallop a little? I would love to let my hair down and let the wind blow through my hair," she said then thought *just as it did when I was a little girl riding with Daddy.*

"Sure. Although there is no wind," Tyler replied.

Lady started barking and ran into the woods. "She's probably chasing a squirrel. I didn't see any deer around."

"Does she chase deer? Aren't you afraid she might get kicked in the head by one?"

"I don't think she could catch up to them. Have you ever seen them jump over fences?"

"Yes, I have. I guess you're right. I wouldn't want to see Lady get hurt," she answered sincerely.

"That's sweet of you. You just met Lady and already you are concerned about her."

"Oh, now you're laughing at me. You think I'm a softy. I love most animals."

CHAPTER 10

Tyler pulled his horse to a halt next to what appeared to be woods. Sarah pulled up next to him and they both dismounted. "What is here?" Sarah asked.

"This is where we are going to picnic," he replied.

"In the woods?" Sarah asked curiously.

"You'll see," he said taking her hand and leading her down a path and out into a clearing.

"Oh my gosh! What a perfect place for a picnic," she said, running over to a big grassy area by an old oak tree. "Tyler, is this lake part of your property?"

"Yes, it is. Here, help me spread out this cloth," he said handing her one end of what looked like a light bedspread.

"I'm in awe. What a beautiful sight," she said with her mouth partially open and her eyes shining. Tyler brought the picnic bag and set it down on the spread.

"This is my special place. Sometimes I come up here just to sit and think about things. When I was a teenager my friends and I would come and skinny dip in this lake. My grandpa loved having us."

"I feel flattered that you brought me to your special place. What kind of things do you think about?" she asked.

"Mostly my future like marriage, children and business. I also reminisce about my childhood days with my grandfather."

"So this was your grandfather's place. Did you inherit it? Were you his only grandchild?"

"No, I have an older brother and sister and yes, I did inherit the farm and the horses. Most of the furniture belonged to my grandparents also."

"Didn't your siblings feel . . . you know . . . cheated?"

"He wanted me to have it. He gave the others money, which pleased them more. He came over here from Scotland and joined with his partner from the old country and they were extremely successful with their own accounting firm. As a small boy I visited this farm often. I loved it more than any of my other siblings. As I got older, I came over every weekend and worked with my grandpa. He saw how I loved the farm as much as he did and made it known to everyone that it was to be mine when he was gone."

"It's such a wonderful place. I noticed the MacAulay crest above the fireplace. Dulce something . . ."

"Dulce periculum," he interrupted. "It means 'danger is sweet.'"

"Did your grandfather put it there?"

"Yes, and to his memory I have decided it will always be there as long as I own the farm. The family badge is a riding boot. It fit in with my grandpa's love of horses."

"What about your grandmother? Did she come over here with him?"

"Yes. Her name was Elizabeth but he called her Lizzie. She died when I was about twelve, but I always remember some of the expressions she used that nobody understood, except Grandpa."

"Like what?" she asked. She was captivated by his family history. She didn't feel like she had one.

"She would say things like 'Bob's your uncle'; 'Your room looks like Anakin's midden' if it was a mess; and 'It's a cold country wanting a shirt and a cold country with one,'" he answered shrugging his shoulders.

"You never found out what they all meant?"

"I think the cold country saying sounds like maybe Scotland whether it gets a shirt or not is still a cold country. Grandpa said Anakin's midden referred to a meat factory that at the end of the week would throw out food that they didn't sell and the poor people of Glasgow would line up to get some of it. That was a long time ago. Like I think in the 1920's. A midden is where you put garbage."

"When did your grandpa die?"

"I had just entered college when his health got bad. I was glad he lived close enough for me to be able to come and see him often. We had some of our more intimate talks then. I promised him that I would take good care of the farm and raise his great grandchildren here. One day I will take my children to his hometown of Dumbarton in Scotland and tell them of him."

"How long after that did he die?"

"About three years."

She was silent for a moment then she said, "Kincaid is a Scottish name also. The badge is a triple tower castle with an arm coming from the middle tower with a sword in hand. The motto is 'This I Defend,'" Sarah said. "That's all my dad told me."

"I wonder if Kevin knows that?" Tyler inquired. "He knows my grandpa was from Scotland. He knew him, but he never mentioned his name was Scottish."

"Don't you think your grandpa would have known Kincaid was Scottish?"

"I don't know. Maybe he and Kevin talked about it and I just didn't know it."

"If you think about it, you might ask Kevin," Sarah suggested. "I would be interested to see if he knows anything more."

Tyler opened the picnic bag and brought out the food. Sarah thoroughly enjoyed the chicken lunch and told him she thought he was a good cook. After lunch, they relaxed on the blanket enjoying the warm sun. After a while Sarah sat up to enjoy the view. She gazed out at the lake enjoying the total serenity of the place. Tyler couldn't take his eyes off her and saw tears in her eyes.

"Sarah, what's wrong?"

"Tyler, I have never been happier. Ever since I left home, life has been full of new positive experiences for me. I was so held back from showing my real personality that you can't imagine how wonderful it is to get to know myself. I love to laugh and tease but as a child I had no one to tease or laugh with. I have met so many people that enjoy being my friend. You were a very special person to me as a child and I wasn't sure that I would ever see you again and here I am sitting looking out at your lake enjoying a wonderful picnic with you.

He knew she was enjoying his grandpa's farm almost as much as he did. The other girls he had brought to the farm when his grandpa was still alive, didn't show much interest in it at all.

"If I would not have made the decision to leave Marshallville and venture out on my own, I would have ended up like my mother. I feel so sorry for her, Tyler. She has missed out on all the beautiful experiences life has to offer." She shared with him the fact that her father had a lady friend.

"She is the only person he confides in. He can't share his feelings with Mom. She thinks that kind of stuff is nonsense."

"It sounds like she has buried a lot of stuff inside," Tyler said.

"My father would have loved her had she let him. I know what it's like to be lonely. He needed her love and she didn't give it. I'm not sure what is going to happen to their marriage, especially now that I'm gone. He only stayed with her because of me."

He put his arm around her. He didn't know what to do for her. His parents had always shown love for each other. He wanted to let her know she was loved. She laid her head on his chest. He rested his back against a tree and sat holding her.

Finally he tilted her head towards him and asked, "Sarah, can I kiss you?"

She was a little nervous. She hoped she wouldn't disappoint him. This was a crucial moment to her. He had to like it! He just had to. She lifted her lips to his. He was slow and tender with his kiss. Sarah felt her head reeling. She returned his kiss trying not to seem too anxious. Was she dreaming? Was her lips really pressed against Tyler MacAulay's? His arm was around her waist supporting her. She felt like she must weigh a ton on his arm, as she was so weak she gave no support to herself. He was strong. His arm didn't even shake. When he stopped he brought his head back and looked straight into her eyes. He had a strange look in his eyes. *Was it love?* she thought.

She wondered if he saw the same thing in hers. She certainly knew that was what she was feeling. They got back on the horses and rode back to the house. Sarah enjoyed the short gallop that she had on Sandy.

CHAPTER 11

Kevin Kincaid was out on the golf course early. It was going to be a hot day so it was planned that he and his partner should start early. His golf partner was Tyler's brother, Conor MacAulay. It was the first time they had gotten together for a game in three years. It was one of the things that Kevin missed most during the time he lived in New York. Before he left they would try and get together at least twice or more a month but Conor's wife, Sheila, was not too happy with them getting together more than twice. "The only time we really have as a family is on the weekends," she had complained. They agreed that they would play no more than two Saturday mornings a month. "Kevin, I love having you back but please don't take Conor away *every* Saturday," she had teased when welcoming him back.

By the time they got to the eighth hole Kevin couldn't keep it back. "I think your brother's in love," he said impishly.

"Tyler? You're kidding. We were all beginning to wonder about his sexual preference if you know what I mean," Conor said winking at Kevin. Conor was always joking and loved to tease Tyler. "He dated frequently when he lived here before moving to San Francisco, but he never did bring any of his dates home to meet the family. Are you sure?"

"I am pretty sure. When he saw her last night he went into zombie mode. Mouth open, staring at her like she was an angel straight from heaven."

"Who is she? If he just met her last night how could he be in love? That's not like Tyler."

"Oh, he met her before when he was in grade school."

"Grade school? Didn't she go to high school with him too?"

"No! By the time she got to high school, he was in college. The last time he saw her she was about thirteen and he had just graduated high school," Kevin continued to tease.

"So she's five years younger than him. You don't hang around with little girls five years younger than you in school."

"He didn't hang around with her. He just knew her because of me and he always felt sorry for her."

"He felt sorry for her? Surely, she isn't that bad. Not if Tyler fell head over heels in love with her. How did he know her because of you?"

Kevin didn't answer and took his swing.

"Come on now. I know what you are doing. You're trying to get me unfocused so you can win." Conor was getting frustrated with Kevin by now.

"Okay Conor, she's my cousin Sarah Kincaid. Maybe it is just fascination at this point but he sure is attracted to her."

"Sarah Kincaid? Did you ever tell me you had a cousin? How could an ugly son of a gun like you have a cousin that would knock the socks off Tyler?"

"I am sure you will meet her. This one, I believe, is gonna meet the family," said Kevin convincingly.

"I'm just glad she's female."

"Come on Connor, Tyler has never shown himself to be anything but a real guy."

"I know. I just love to tease him. I'm looking forward to meeting Sarah. I can't wait to call Mom and let her know."

"You're just jealous of him because he is not married and can play golf as many times as he likes . . . only kidding. You know I love Sheila like my own sister."

Conor picked up the phone and dialed his folks. "Hello!" his mom sang into the phone.

"Good news, Mom. Tyler has a girlfriend.

"I am happy to hear he has a girl. I wonder if he will bring this one to meet us?" his mother asked.

"I think he might. She is Kevin Kincaid's cousin and according to him, Tyler went gaga when he met her at the restaurant last night.

"Well let's not jump to any conclusions. We will just have to wait and see."

"Oh, I believe my partner. Tyler is *off* the market."

"Off the what?"

"Never mind, Mom. Are you going to call Tyler and do some snooping?"

"Of course not," she said, sounding as though she would never do such a thing.

"Uh Huh," was all he said.

"Well thanks for calling and letting us know. I'm happy for him but like I said, we will just have to wait and see. 'Bye Conor. I'll talk to you later," she said and hung up.

After she hung up the phone she ran into the family room where Ian was watching Food Network on the television. Ian loved to cook and was a Food Network addict. That suited Alice just fine. It was enjoyable to have someone else do the cooking sometimes. Just having to think of what to cook every day was a chore in itself.

"Ian, isn't it wonderful, Tyler apparently has a girlfriend and according to Conor, he fell head over heels for her. We have to invite them to dinner next weekend so we can meet her."

"Hold on, Alice. Tyler hasn't even told us about her yet. We have to wait until he feels it is time," Ian replied. Alice already had it in her mind to call Tyler later that evening and try and get information from him. She couldn't wait to see this new girl. Being Kevin's cousin made it sound even better since their whole family loved Kevin as another son and brother.

CHAPTER 12

By the time they rode back to the barn and took care of the horses and put them away, it was about three o'clock. Tyler made some ice tea and they went out to sit on the porch.

"The day that I called you in San Francisco was such a disappointment for me. I wanted so much to have you show me around. I went out by myself and walked around Fisherman's Wharf . . ."

"And you were the beautiful woman I couldn't take my eyes off of at the restaurant. I still can't get over that."

"The reason I smiled back at you was because I saw a resemblance to the Tyler I knew ten years earlier. But you said you had to catch a plane, so I thought it was just someone who might look like you."

"I did have to catch a plane but I took a client out to lunch to go over some final papers with him before going to the airport," he said. Then grinning, "I think we are destined for each other." She loved his sense of humor, and his wicked little smile when he would tease her. She loved his personality and the apparent self-confidence that he exuded. All the years that she had thought about him never prepared her for the man that he was. He was the most handsome, strongest man she had ever seen. He was about six feet tall or more; that was perfect for her five feet nine height. His skin was tanned and his blue eyes seemed to look right into her like he could see her soul. He seemed to be very comfortable with himself. His medium brown hair was thick and he had the most beautiful smile, exposing almost perfect teeth.

"Earth to Sarah!"

She snapped back to reality. "I'm sorry!" she said embarrassed. She didn't realize she had spent so much staring at him. They sat quietly for a few moments then Sarah surprised Tyler when she said, "When I was going to school in Marshallville I could never have believed my life would turn out like this. I really owe it to you, Tyler."

"What do you mean you owe it to me? You were the one that studied hard to get that scholarship to college and then you worked real hard to take care of yourself. Sarah, I know the background you came from and I can't tell you how impressed I am at what you've accomplished. How can you give me praise for that?"

"You probably don't remember, but when I was about eight and the kids were teasing me about the way I was dressed and all, you came and sat beside me and encouraged me. You told me that the girls were jealous because I was so pretty. Nobody had ever told me that before. You also said that when I was older I could dress the way I wanted and do whatever I wanted. That stuck with me and I pondered what you said many times, wondering what I would do. A number of years later, I realized what I was going to do to change my life. I would work hard for that scholarship and put myself through college and get a good paying job then figure my life from that point. When you said those words to me that day, I knew that when I grew up I was going to marry you." She laughed.

He was captivated by what she was saying until she laughed which brought him back to reality and he laughed also. "There were many times, Sarah, when I thought about that little girl. I would wonder how she was doing and if there was someone else who would encourage her."

"Only you did Tyler and I'm truly thankful. I don't know what I would have done if I hadn't held on to your words."

"Tell me about your friends now," he said.

"When I first came to Austin, I was afraid. I was going to be sharing a room with two girls I had never met. But Trish and Lisa turned out to be my best friends. Trish is the one I traveled to San Francisco with."

"You must have gone through an amazing transformation."

"Before I left Marshallville I bought some new clothes and got a new hairstyle but the job I was supposed to be getting fell through, and the person who interviewed me sent me to the Canto Modeling Agency. His friend was the owner. He immediately gave me a job and they really went to work on me. I didn't recognize myself."

"I bet all the college guys were dying to date you," Tyler said curious to know of her past dates.

"I had a couple of guy friends but I had no time to date. Besides I was more interested in learning to be a best friend. It was fun learning to do all the girly things I never knew about," she said laughing. "At the agency, Gloria was my best friend. I still call her occasionally, but she travels a lot. What about you, who took care of your farm while you lived in San Francisco?"

"My parents moved from Marshallville when my grandfather got ill. They moved in with him for a while and after he died they stayed for about two more years while they were having their own home built in Austin. For the next few years they would check on it. Especially Dad."

"How did your dad feel about the farm?" she asked.

"He loved it but he wanted something a little more easy to take care of."

They sat talking for a few hours getting caught up with each other's life when Sarah looked at her watch.

"It's six o'clock already. I should be going."

"Well at least let's have dinner together."

"I'm really not very hungry after all the chicken I ate. It was marvelous."

"How about soup and salad?"

"Great!"

They watched a movie and then Sarah decided it really was time to go. He walked her out to her car. As she drove away she felt extremely disappointed that he hadn't arranged for another date. She thought everything was going real well. He had even kissed her. She had hoped he would want to see her the next day. "Maybe he already had plans," she said aloud to herself

After she left Tyler called his mom. "Hello," Alice MacAulay said into the phone.

"Hi mom! Can I bring a friend to dinner tomorrow after church?" Tyler asked.

Alice was more than surprised. Ian thought she was rushing things by wanting to have them over next weekend, but here was Tyler asking to bring her over tomorrow. She pretended not to know who it was.

"Sure son. Is it Kevin?"

"No, it's his cousin Sarah. I want you to meet her."

"You're barely home a week and you've found a girl you want the family to meet? This is most unusual for you, Tyler. What's going on?"

"I feel good about this girl. I think I'm falling in love with her."

"Oh! Well, by all means bring her. We'll all be dying of curiosity."

She hung up the phone and immediately went to find her husband.

"Ian, Tyler just called. Guess what? He wants to bring her over tomorrow for dinner. I'll have to call everyone and let them know," she said then ran back out of the room to the phone.

Sarah dealt with the disappointment all the way home. If he were interested he would have asked to see her again. He didn't even mention it. What a terrible way to end a perfect day. As she put her key in the door she heard the phone ring. Turning it quickly and pushing the door open, she ran for the phone. *It just has to be Tyler,* she thought. "Hello!" she said in an almost too expecting voice.

"Sarah, Tyler here," he said as though she didn't know it was him. "I would like you to meet my family. I know it sounds so soon . . ."

"I would love to meet your family Tyler," she said almost hysterically. "When?"

"We always get together for Sunday dinner after church, I would like to invite you tomorrow."

Church! She hadn't thought about the fact that he might be involved in a church. That bothered her. After all that is what caused all her troubles as a child. "Will you pick me up after your church service?" she asked.

"Sure, I'll pick you up around twelve-thirty," he said.

CHAPTER 13

Alice thought a casual meal would make the girl feel more at ease so she opted for a cookout. Their daughter Fiona and her husband Larry and Conor and his wife Sheila would be there also.

Everyone was there when Tyler and Sarah arrived. Sarah had worn a short cotton sundress. Not too short, just above the knees. It was green with pink and yellow flowers. The green helped to enhance her green eyes. She wore white open-toe flat sandals. After giving his mom a hug and shaking hands with his dad, Tyler made the introductions. "Everyone, this is Sarah." Then he took her around and introduced her to each member of the family. Alice MacAulay fussed over Sarah, trying to make sure she was comfortable. She was a petite blonde woman around sixty. Fiona said she was so happy to meet her and that she was glad her brother had met such a nice girl. Sarah could see a likeness to Tyler, but she took after her mom when it came to height. Ian MacAulay was tall, over six feet with gray thick hair and had the most mischievous blue eyes she had ever seen. He told her that she was too pretty for his son. "Just joking of course. His mother and I are very proud of him."

Tyler then introduced her to Conor. "This is my brother Conor and his wife Sheila."

"Hello, Sarah. I'm Kevin's golf partner. If he's out golfing, he will more than likely be with me."

"Yes. You're lucky Tyler isn't as addicted as those two," chimed in Sheila.

Conor was slightly shorter than Tyler but there was some resemblance. *Kevin totally underrated his cousin. She was stunning. How did old Tyler do it?* he wondered. Conor and Sheila had two children, Murray who was eight and Leslie who was six. They were playing with the MacAulay's two dogs, Zeke and Jake, both Golden Retrievers. "Are you going to be our aunt?" Leslie asked.

"She can only be our aunt if she is married to Tyler. They've just met. Don't ask silly questions," Murray told her.

"Well, Leslie we'll just wait and see," Tyler said.

Sarah felt herself blushing and noticed Tyler grinning at her. She hoped no one else had seen. Alice MacAulay saw and it pleased her that Sarah could blush. It didn't take long for Sarah to be at ease and after a while was talking and laughing freely with the rest of the family. Alice MacAulay spent as much time as she could with her trying to find out as much as possible. Tyler told them how he had seen her in a restaurant in San Francisco and how he was so attracted to her not knowing at the time that it was Sarah until she walked into the Irish Pub two nights ago.

"What a coincidence," said Alice, amazed that they could have seen one another in a city so far away.

"Actually, I knew Tyler was there. Kevin told me the name of the company he worked for," admitted Sarah, a little guiltily. "My best friend was moving there so I went with her and contacted Tyler but he was leaving for Austin, so I went sightseeing and went into a restaurant at Fisherman's Wharf and Tyler happened to be there."

"I just saw this beautiful young woman walk into the restaurant and I couldn't take my eyes off her. We didn't know one another since we hadn't seen each other in about ten years. To have her walk into my life a second time was more than coincidental to me. I think it's destiny."

"Well I think so too, sweetheart," agreed his mom.

"I did have a little part in making it happen. I went to San Francisco with intentions of contacting him, but choosing the same restaurant and both being attracted to someone we didn't think we knew . . . well that sounds like more than coincidence," she admitted again. "Also, I did play a hand in getting together with them at the Irish Pub. Since I knew both he and Kevin had moved back, I called Kevin."

"However you guys met doesn't matter, we are just happy that you did," said Conor and everyone agreed. He made sure he got Tyler aside to let him know how lucky he ought to feel. Sarah had a wonderful time with his family and felt totally at ease with them all. They left first because Tyler knew the family would want to have a meeting to see what everyone thought of this new girl that might become the latest in-law. Not that it mattered. Tyler already had formed his plans.

After they left, everyone talked about how genuine she was. "When she first walked in and I saw what a beauty she was, I was sure she was going to be snotty to Sheila and me," said Fiona, "but she was so much fun. Smart too! Nothing about her relates to a bimbo."

"It's funny how we relate being a bimbo to someone who looks great and has a great body." Sheila said and Fiona nodded her head in agreement.

"Did you know she is an engineer? She graduated from University of Texas with top honors and put herself through school by modeling," said Alice obviously happy for her boy. "She's had her picture on the cover of a few magazines, which I have to find," she continued. "I am very impressed with this young lady and have you ever seen Tyler look so happy?" she asked her husband.

"Who wouldn't be grinning with a beauty like that on your arm?" Ian said grinning at Conor and Larry.

"Oh, all you men see is the outside of a woman," complained Alice.

"No sweetie, I agree she is a very intelligent and unobtrusive young lady. She would fit real nicely into this family."

"Now you're sounding like Leslie. Give her a chance to get used to this lot," Fiona said.

"I have to say, that when Tyler called and asked if he could bring Sarah, I was a little concerned. After all, they only got together for the first time on Friday night," Alice admitted

"He told me that they spent the whole day at his place riding and doing a lot of talking." Ian said. "He almost sounds like he knows she's the one. I don't think there will be a long engagement here."

After they had been dating a little more than a week, seeing each other every night, Sarah's curiosity got the better of her. "Tyler, why did you take me to meet your family so soon?"

"Sarah, I have very strong feelings for you. I'm not one to rush into anything but I want to marry you. I don't know when but I do. Will you marry me, Sarah?" She sat staring at him as though she didn't hear him.

"What . . . what did you say?"

"I asked you to marry me."

"Tyler I have known all my life I wanted to be your wife but I didn't expect you to ask me after one week. Are you sure that's what you want."

"I am positive."

"Then the answer is yes . . . yes," she squealed and jumped into his arms.

"Please arrange a time to take me to meet your folks."

After taking Sarah home Tyler couldn't wait to call his folks. Ian answered the phone.

"Dad, I asked Sarah to marry me and she said yes. We're not sure when but we know we will."

"Tyler, this is awfully fast, but I trust you on this. I believe in my heart you know without a doubt that Sarah is the girl for you."

"Wait! Don't hang up," Alice yelled coming into the room. She had heard Ian's side of the conversation. Grabbing the phone she said,

"Are you sure about this, Tyler?"

"Yes! What did the family think of her?" Tyler asked.

"We all thought very well of her. She is a lovely young woman, but *we* are not marrying her. Marriage is a big commitment."

"It is but I've never felt like committing to anyone else. This is the first woman I've ever felt this way about. I love her personality, her sincerity and she is not bad to look at either.

"Well nobody will argue with you on that note. If you *are* sure, you'd better call Pastor Jones and schedule some meetings for marriage counseling, especially if you are planning on marrying soon. I'm not sure how many weeks he likes to schedule before marrying a couple."

"Mom, we are not going to have a large wedding but I will set up the meetings. I'll call him in the morning."

"What do you think, Ian?" Alice asked her husband after hanging up the phone.

"They are not teenagers. I think they are mature enough to know this is what they want," he answered. "Frankly I was real impressed with the intelligence and maturity of Sarah."

"But don't you think they should date a while longer and make sure?"

"He told me that last Saturday when they went horseback riding, that they spent almost the whole day talking about important things about themselves. I think that they have opened up to one another in the short time they've known each other than some couples do in years of knowing each other, but not really knowing each other, if you know what I mean."

"You're talking in riddles but I do know what you mean and I believe you're right about Tyler and Sarah. I'm just a little nervous about the speed he's going at," Alice confessed.

"When you know she's the girl, you just want to get that ring on her finger," Ian said squeezing his wife teasingly.

Sarah had tried to set up a time to take Tyler home to meet her parents but her mother always had excuses. Finally, Sarah decided she would call her dad and tell him they were coming. If her mother wanted to stay up in her room, so be it. At least she would have tried. Two weeks after meeting Tyler's family, Sarah took Tyler home to meet hers. When they arrived at her parent's home Sarah was surprised to see her mother there. She was very polite but distant. She asked Tyler if he attended church.

"Yes ma'am. I was raised in the Baptist church. My family all attend and Sarah came with us this morning." Tyler had talked to Sarah about the differences between his church and her mother's so she finally gave in and went with him. She was actually quite comfortable with it.

"I am happy to hear that Sarah," said her father, meaning he was happy that she was getting involved in a regular church. Her mother, on the other hand, said nothing and looked even more distant. She busied herself in the kitchen making coffee and bringing out finger foods. Sarah knew Tyler was feeling nervous. They weren't sure how her dad would feel about their commitment to marriage after such a short dating period.

"Mr. and Mrs. Kincaid, I love your daughter very much and would like to ask for her hand in marriage," Tyler said. Sarah had talked to John about Tyler and he knew she really liked him but he was not prepared for this. Her mother sat there looking confused. She didn't know if she was happy or not. This would be final. There would be no chance of Sarah coming back to her. She will belong to someone else.

"All I can ask is, are you both very sure of this decision? It is a big step and I don't want my daughter to suffer the pain of divorce."

"We are as sure as we can be, sir," Tyler said.

"I am very sure there is nobody else that I would be happier with, Daddy."

"I don't mean to be disrespectful, Tyler," John said "but we really don't know you or your family."

"You're right sir, would you both like to come to dinner at my house and I will arrange for my family to come? That way you can meet them and judge for yourselves."

"I would like that, Tyler. It's not that I don't trust you with my daughter, I believe in Sarah's judgment of people, but I just think it appropriate that we meet them."

"You are perfectly right, sir and I know my parents would agree with you. How would tomorrow afternoon be? We try to get together for dinner often after church."

John turned to Olivia who just shrugged her shoulders. "I think that would be good for us. What time?"

"Would two o'clock be suitable?"

"Yes! Thank you, Tyler, we'll be there."

On the way out of town, Sarah showed Tyler the church that she attended with her mother.

"I knew it was this one. People at the Baptist church used to pray for the people that attended it," he said.

"Why were they praying for them? I mean what did they know about the church?" she questioned.

"Before my parents moved to Austin, my dad was an elder at the Baptist Church. The name of your mom's church indicates that they believe they are the *only* people of God. That always brings suspicion."

"I never even thought about that, but I suppose you're right."

"My dad and another elder visited the church a couple of times. I heard my dad telling my mom that the pastor didn't read from the Bible, but instead would take the teachings of Christ and change them to fit in with his own teachings."

"And what were they?" she questioned again.

"I don't remember too much. But my dad and the other elder also attended an adult class and I do remember he said women had to obey their husband's wishes unless the husband was a heathen. That would be someone who was not part of their church."

"Like my father?"

"Yes. Women with a non-believing husband were told that divorce from a heathen husband was acceptable."

"How come you never told me this before?" questioned Sarah.

"I didn't want you to think I was criticizing it, since your mom still goes there." They were silent for a few seconds then Tyler said, "I don't think your mom is strange or anything. I just think she is insecure in herself. Also the bad things that happened to her as a child had to leave scars. I think she is a nice lady."

She was thinking about what he had said. It made her feel angry that they considered her father a heathen.

"Did you hear me?"

"Oh! I'm sorry," she said bringing her mind back to him. "Thanks! I appreciate that. I was a little uneasy having you meet her."

He just patted her hand. He knew she loved her mother but it was hard because she didn't know how her mother would behave towards him or if she would even come downstairs and meet him. In the short time that they had really known each other, they drew very close.

As soon as they got back to his house he called his parents. Once again Ian answered the phone.

"Dad, can you ask Mom if she can get the family together for dinner at my place tomorrow?"

"What's the occasion son and why such short notice?" Ian inquired.

"Mr. Kincaid would like to meet my family before he gives us his blessing."

"Well here's your mom," he said handing the phone to Alice and whispering Tyler's request in her ear.

"Tyler, did you go and ask the Kincaids for their daughter's hand in marriage without letting them meet us first?" she asked. "You're running into this so fast you aren't even thinking properly."

"I know Mom. You're right. I wasn't thinking."

"Okay, I'm sure everyone will be there but it is really your dad and I that they probably want to meet."

Tyler could hardly wait for the church service to end so that he could go home and make sure everything was okay. Sarah was going back with him to help. He had put together a couple of dishes of lasagna so that all they needed was to be put in the oven. His mind was far from Pastor Jones' sermon this particular morning. This could be the most important day of his life. Mr. Kincaid just had to like him and his family. Of course Tyler didn't know what a gentle man John Kincaid really was and how much he loved his daughter and would do anything for her happiness. The service ended and Tyler grabbed Sarah's hand and started down the aisle.

"See you later guys. We've got to go and get things ready."

"Look at him," Alice said laughing. "He's acting like a married man already."

"He's nervous," said Conor. "Everything has to go perfect for him today."

"So that means be on your best behavior Conor," Fiona teased.

Sarah was tearing up lettuce and chopping vegetables for a salad. It felt very comfortable to her to be in the kitchen helping prepare a meal. She truly loved the house and was getting a taste of what it would be like when she became Mrs. MacAulay and this would be her home. The Kincaids were the first to arrive. They were impressed.

"Is this *your* home Tyler?" John asked.

"Yes. It was my grandfather's. I inherited it. If you like I can give you a tour."

"No, I'm sure your folks will be here soon. It smells good," said John looking around at the house. He was impressed already with Tyler. In fact he immediately liked him when he went to their home to ask for Sarah's hand. He knew he was a well-bred boy and would treat Sarah well. Shortly after they got there, the MacAulay clan arrived. Tyler introduced them all around.

"Mr. and Mrs. Kincaid my son is so head over heels in love with your daughter that he wasn't thinking when he went to your home to ask for her hand, without properly having a meeting with both of the families," Alice said apologetically.

"That's okay, please call us John and Olivia. We understood his condition, didn't we Olivia?"

"Yes, we did," she said in her usual polite but quiet manner. They socialized for a while then Tyler asked everyone into the dining room. After they were all seated, he and Sarah brought in the food then they took their own seats.

"This is the first time I've eaten in this room," he told everyone.

"Maybe after you and Sarah get married you can have us all over more often," Conor blurted out. His wife gave him a stern look.

"We haven't got everyone's consent yet, Conor." Tyler said embarrassed.

"Well, you certainly have *our* consent," John said rather loudly smiling at Tyler. "Anyone who would go to all this trouble to impress his future in-laws proves that he really must love their daughter," John said raising his glass. "Congratulations, Tyler and Sarah." Everyone joined in the congratulations and breathed a sigh of relief.

"Daddy, you knew all along you were going to consent and you had poor Tyler worried."

"I did know when I first met him but I still thought it proper for us to meet his family and for them to meet us."

"You were perfectly correct, John," Alice chimed in. They talked together for quite a while. John fit right in with Alice and Ian MacAulay.

"I'm really happy for Sarah. Tyler is a fine young man. I'm also happy that she is going to be a part of a wonderful family," John told Ian and Alice.

"We all fell in love with Sarah as soon as we met her and already consider her part of our family," Ian said.

John could see that Olivia had reached her socialization level. Standing up he said, "Sweetheart, I think it's time your momma and I head back home." Sarah understood. This had been a long time for Olivia to be in a situation where she was expected to have conversations with people she didn't know.

"Thank you both for coming and thank you for your blessing on our marriage," she said, kissing them both on the cheek. Tyler got up and shook hands with John.

"Thank you. I don't know what I'd have done if you wouldn't have given your consent."

"How could I not Tyler, you have a wonderful family and I know you'll be good to her."

"Sarah tells me you like horses. I'd love to have you come back soon and go horseback riding," Tyler said then almost like an afterthought he continued, "would you like to see the horses before you leave?"

"Not now, but I'd love to come back soon and go riding with you. I'll see them at that time." John knew Olivia would be upset if he left her alone with the family. Everyone said their goodbyes to the Kincaids and shortly after they left, the MacAulays also left.

When they were alone, Tyler said to Sarah, "I enjoyed having you co-host with me. I can't wait to have you here all the time."

"I kept thinking pretty soon I will be making memories with you in this lovely house."

CHAPTER 14

The next two months were extremely busy for Tyler and Sarah. Besides their jobs, they were doing marriage counseling with Pastor Jones two nights a week. They would meet at the church and have a one-hour session, and then they would eat out. Preparing for their wedding took up much of their time also. Wedding invitations had to be chosen, then sent out and a list had to be made to make sure they didn't miss anyone. Sarah was thankful to have Alice MacAulay's help. She helped Sarah pick out the invitations; she helped prepare the list of people who would be invited to the reception; she worked with the wedding coordinator at the church, letting her know of the music, the flower arrangements, anything that had to do with the church; and she arranged for the reception at a lovely hotel that had a banquet room. Sarah didn't know what she would have done without her. Alice was like her personal assistant and then of course there was Gloria, who helped her pick out the dress and the bridesmaids' dresses. It was the busiest time and most exciting time of Sarah's life.

After a month of counseling, Pastor Jones was positive that Tyler and Sarah were right for each other. He was truly impressed with their honesty and forthrightness and their obvious love and devotion to one another. He shook their hands and told them that he would be more than honored to join them in holy matrimony. She was thrilled, when a few weeks before the wedding, Mark from Canto Agency told her as a gift he would be more than happy to do her makeup and Cathie said she would do her hair and Paul offered also as a gift to be her wedding photographer. She certainly couldn't ask for better than that trio. As far as Sarah was concerned, they were the best in the field. What a gift. Cathie also gave Sarah a bottle of her favorite hair conditioner.

"Make sure you use it every day from now until your wedding day and your hair will be healthy and shiny."

"Thanks Cathie. I appreciate what you're doing for me so much," Sarah said taking the bottle of conditioner.

"I would be jealous if you got someone else to do your hair. Also let's set up a date and time for us to go over various styles."

"I have a hairstyle in mind. Maybe we can go through some of the pictures that Paul took of me, because I remember a hairstyle where you swept my hair up and I thought it looked quite elegant."

On the evening of the wedding rehearsal, Sarah was actually surprised when her mom showed up with her dad at the MacAulay's home where they had been instructed to go. Alice MacAulay had called and given Olivia the directions to her home and invited her and her husband to stay the night with them. Olivia had thanked her for her kindness but thought that they would be staying with their daughter.

After the rehearsal everyone went to the MacAulay home for the rehearsal dinner. Olivia continued to be polite and answer questions but never asked any. She thought it rude to ask too many questions of people you were not familiar with. When Sarah and her parents were ready to leave, Alice made sure everyone knew the plan.

"Sarah, your hairdresser and makeup artist are going to be here around eleven o'clock, so what time do you think you should be here?"

"I'll be here at ten-thirty," she answered.

"The wedding is at one o'clock. John and Olivia, you are more than welcome to come over with Sarah. We can have breakfast," Alice offered.

"Thank you Alice," John said "but I think we're going to do a little touring around Austin. It has been a long time since we've been here." Actually he thought that Alice would have enough to do without fussing over two more guests.

"I don't blame you. It will be a zoo around here. Well we will be leaving for the church at twelve-fifteen and Olivia you will be riding with us. John of course will be with the bride."

As Alice and Ian walked them to the door John turned and shook Alice's hand and said "Alice, Olivia and I want to thank you for making reception arrangements. I don't know what we would have done without you. Also for everything else you helped Sarah with."

"Yes," said Olivia. "Thank you very much," she said and reached out her hand to Alice. Sarah and John gave one another a surprised look but of course said nothing.

Like Alice predicted, it was a zoo in her house the day of the wedding. Mark and Cathie had come together in Mark's car. They were working on her makeup and hair. They were so skilled they knew how to work together without getting in one another's way. Gloria arrived at eleven-thirty to help Sarah on with her dress and hairpiece. Gloria looked lovely in her lavender bridesmaids dress, she had helped Sarah to pick them out also and it was very flattering on her. Trish and Lisa arrived at twelve o'clock, at the same time as Sarah's parents and the rest of the MacAulays.

Mark and Cathie went downstairs since their work was done. Cathie had been very pleased with the way Sarah's hair had turned out. She swept it up in the back and left a wispy stray lock on each side of her face. It had a casual elegant look. Mark, of course, had done a great job with the makeup. It was so different from when he applied her makeup for a shoot. This time it was very light but still gave her face a wonderful glow.

When Gloria finished putting on the hairpiece, the three bridesmaids stood back and stared at Sarah in disbelief. Her dress was a simple yet beautiful white silk that flowed softly over the curves of her body then gently flared out at her ankles. Her hairpiece was a simple pearl headband with little flower studs sprinkled around her hair. She wore a single strand of pearls and pearl studs in her ears.

"Sarah," Gloria said admiring her, "all I can say is you are simply elegant."

"Looking at you makes me want to cry," said Trish. "I just remember that shy girl that walked into Mrs. Sullivan's boarding house a little more than four years ago."

"I was thinking the same thing," said Lisa.

John Kincaid knocked on the door to let the girls know that their limousine was waiting downstairs for them. They opened the door and stepped out.

"Go see your baby girl, Mr. Kincaid," Gloria said opening the door wider. Tears did come to John Kincaid's eyes when he saw his daughter, then Gloria motioned the other two girls downstairs.

"Excuse me, Sarah. I knew I would feel emotional when I saw you but not this emotional," he said wiping his eyes with a Kleenex. "You are absolutely beautiful. Tyler is a very lucky man."

Everyone was seated when John and Sarah arrived at the church. Gloria, Trish and Lisa were waiting in the foyer with the wedding planner, Mrs. Logan. The organist started playing and Mrs. Logan motioned the bridesmaids over to the door. Lisa was first, then Trish, then Gloria. As each girl walked down the aisle they could hear the congregation breathing a sigh of appreciation. They also saw the big smile on Tyler's face as he watched them come towards him. After they had taken their place on the platform opposite the groomsmen, who were Kevin, Conor and another of Tyler's friends named Andrew, the organist started to play loudly "Here Comes the Bride." Everyone stood up and turned to look down the aisle to get a glimpse of the bride. As Sarah came to the door on her father's arm, the people who could see her gave a loud gasp. The gasp seemed to get louder as more and more people could see her. As she got closer to Tyler she could see the tears in his eyes.

"Who gives this woman to this man in marriage?" Pastor Jones asked.

"Her mother and I do," answered John. Then John took his seat beside Olivia. He was surprised to see how admiringly Olivia was staring at Sarah. When Pastor Jones was finished he introduced the couple. It was the sweetest sound to Sarah's ears.

"I would like to introduce Mr. and Mrs. Tyler MacAulay." Everyone applauded as the bride and groom walked back down the aisle.

After the ceremony Paul took pictures. He was so professional he knew exactly what he wanted to capture and it didn't take him long to get a string of photos he knew would be fantastic. Only the family and wedding party were still in the church. The rest of the people who were invited to the reception went on to the hotel. Everyone was seated at their tables when the banquet hall door opened and Kevin introduced the party.

"The groom's parents, Mr. and Mrs. Ian MacAulay." Alice and Ian walked in and took their place at the table with the bridal party.

"The bride's parents, Mr. and Mrs. John Kincaid." Olivia and John took their place at the bridal table.

"The bride and groom, Mr. and Mrs. Tyler MacAulay." Everyone stood up and cheered as Sarah and Tyler took their place at the table. Toasts were made. Then the food came in.

After the meal the band played and a singer sang *Thanks to the Keeper of the Stars,* a song made popular by country star Tracy Byrd. Tyler had requested this for their first dance. When it came to the lyrics "Now I hold everything when I hold you in my arms . . ." Tyler sang the words in her ear. She smiled up at him as he pulled her closer to him. John and Alice danced and when Ian MacAulay went over to get Olivia up to dance, Sarah thought her mother would faint but she actually got up and tried to dance. When John saw his wife up on the floor with Ian he had to smile. He was proud to see her trying to join in with everyone. John got his daughter up next and told her that he could never be happier than he was that whole day.

"I am sure that you and Tyler are going to have a wonderful life together. He is so good for you darlin'. I couldn't have made a better choice if I had searched the whole earth looking for a suitor for you. He is almost perfect and it is obvious that you love him."

"Thanks Daddy. I do love him very much."

"I'm also very proud of the way your mother has behaved during this time. I know it must be hard for her, but you know Sarah, I think she is enjoying herself. Let's not give up. I have been hoping for a long time."

Everyone had such a wonderful time. Sarah agreed with her dad that even her mom had a good time. She and Tyler had decided to put off a honeymoon to a later date when it was more convenient for them. John had offered to put them up in the hotel where they had the reception but Sarah had said she wanted her wedding night to be spent in the wonderful house that she would call home. Tyler had washed the sheets that morning so their bed would be fresh. He had had a cleaning lady come in the day before and clean the house. He wanted the house to have an open-arms look.

Tyler carried her over the threshold where Lady welcomed them.

"Welcome to your new home, Mrs. MacAulay," Tyler said as he put her down. She reached up to him and kissed him.

"Thank you my wonderful husband," she smiled up at him. "I love this place so much. I can't believe I get to come home here every night."

The next morning as they lay in bed relaxing Sarah said, "You know Tyler, in a way I'm glad I wasn't real popular in school. I may have missed out on a lot of fun but I also missed all the peer pressure that some kids have to put up with."

"I'm glad you waited for me darling. You are very, very special to me," he said leaning over to kiss her.

CHAPTER 15

They were both so busy during the week with their jobs but at the weekend they loved to relax. They felt they didn't have enough time together. Relaxing could be just hanging around the house watching movies, sometimes with Kevin; visiting friends and family; going to dinner and meeting with Kevin and date; going horseback riding at their farm with a picnic and taking a swim in the lake and sometimes they loved just walking in Zilker Park. The Botanical Gardens were beautiful. Both Sarah and Tyler loved the plants and flowers and the pond with the flowers blooming in it. They tried to keep their weekends as relaxing as possible. Sarah's favorite Saturday night was when they stayed home and she would soak for half-an-hour in the tub with her aromatherapy oils by candlelight and soft music. Tyler would come in after she had her half-hour relaxation time and wash her back. Then she would get into something comfortable like her soft leisurewear and they would watch movies that he had rented. They didn't eat dinner on those nights because they loved to snack while watching the movies. Tyler made some great finger foods. That was their perfect Saturday night.

Sarah worked in the Disk Development Department at Carp, Incorporated. The people she worked with had a lot of respect for her. She was an excellent engineer. It hadn't always been like that. When she first started sharing her thoughts at meetings, most of the men didn't pay much attention to her. They thought she was just another pretty face that had squeaked through the system. They used to make jokes about her, talking about her body as though she was using it to get ahead. It wasn't long though before they saw what their boss had seen in her. She was a hands-on, problem-solver. She did whatever it took to find the problem and a solution. She would suit up in a bunny suit and go through the clean room attempting to locate any source of contamination; she would check out the lab and go out on the line making sure that everyone was performing their job properly and making sure procedures were correct. She was kind to her people but she made sure they did everything by the book. John, Sam's boss, noticed right away Sarah's abilities for troubleshooting. Sarah reported directly to a first line manager named Steve, who reported to Sam.

Shortly after she had started working at Carp, John had asked Sarah to work with the other engineers and see if she could help them with a problem. They had spent about a week trying to figure out the reason for the anomalous conditions on hundreds of disks. After spending a whole day trouble-shooting, Sarah told John that she thought she had found the problem. John asked her to set up a meeting for the next afternoon inviting everyone who was involved in the project. At the meeting Sarah presented her findings showing that the problem did not lie with *their* plant but with the plant in North Carolina that produced the substrates. They had miniscule bumps on them. That changed the minds of the male engineers about her and in fact, they would come to her for advice and help after that but not all of them were happy with her. A few of them were jealous. The fact that this barely-out-of-school woman could find the problem when they couldn't, threatened them. Jack Malone was one and Mike Johnson was another and Sarah felt there may have been a few more.

One evening, after they had been married about three weeks she announced to him that she was going to have to travel to France with her co-worker, Sam to help their people over there with a problem. Tyler felt a twinge of jealousy.

"Why you and Sam?"

"Sam and I work out a lot of problems together and our boss, John, felt that we could solve this one faster than anyone else. Sam is a second line manager immediately under John so for me to be chosen to go help him is quite a compliment," Sarah said.

"I just feel funny with you traveling with another guy. Do you stay at the same hotel?"

Sarah smiled at him. "Tyler, we will be so busy by the time we get through working for the day we will want to go straight to our rooms for relaxation and private time. I will never go to the room of any of my co-workers. In fact, whether it is a man or a woman, I will always have the secretary get me a room on a separate floor. After working together all day, I am sure people like to have their quiet time. I know I will. Sam will probably spend most of the evening talking on the phone with his wife."

Tyler felt stupid for being concerned. "I'm sorry, babe. I didn't mean to sound so jealous."

"Don't worry. You will be on my mind the whole time and I will be anxious to get back to you."

She walked over to the stove to see what he had cooked. "This smells great. What is it?"

"It's a Flemish Stew. It's made with beer. The beer gives it a nice rich gravy." Tyler took after his father when it came to cooking. He was good and he enjoyed it.

"Mm! Can't wait to taste it."

"How was your day?"

"It was okay until John told us we were going to France at the end of next week." She handed him a glass of ice tea and sat next to him on the sofa. "I feel like we don't have enough time together as it is. I didn't think my job would include traveling to foreign countries. The other reason I was picked is because I speak French, although I don't see why that would matter since according to Sam the people he works with over there speak English fluently." She became quiet and seemed to be thinking of something.

"What is it?" Tyler asked.

"You know I could swear I was being followed after work today and yesterday," she said.

"Oh yeah? Tell me about it," he said with a concerned look.

"Yesterday when I drove past the guard shack I looked back and noticed a shiny black car pulling out of a parking spot. I didn't give it much thought, but after I was on the highway for about ten minutes, I looked in my rear view mirror and I am sure it was about two cars behind me. Today I happened to look out for it and sure enough it pulled out of the same parking area and was close behind me again."

"Ask your co-workers if someone got a new car. It may just be a coincidence."

"It could be but why would an employee be parked outside of the guard shack? The thing that made me uneasy is that it pulled out right after me both days and today I left work half-an-hour earlier."

"Well if it happens again let me know. I will come down to your work and watch out for it."

CHAPTER 16

Although she knew she would really miss Tyler, she was excited about going to France. Sam had been to Courbevoie before but she had never left the United States and France was one of the countries she always dreamed of visiting. They arrived at the Charles De Gaulle airport on Sunday evening and took a cab to the Best Western George Sand in Courbevoie, an area outside of Paris. The train station was within easy walking distance with trains frequently going into the City of Lights, Sam had told her. The hotel had about 30 rooms with 19-century décor. Sarah called Tyler as soon as she settled into her room. It was nighttime and she could see the lights of the city.

"Tyler, I'm at my hotel. Everything went well."

"Hi! Baby, I'm glad you had a good trip. I miss you already."

"I miss you too. We have got to come back here together. It is *so* romantic."

"We'll put Paris on our agenda."

"Let's make a list of all the things we want to do together and work at making them happen."

"Sounds like a good deal." They talked for about fifteen minutes then she hung up with a promise to call him in a few days and let him know how things were going.

The next day they went to Carp, Incorporated, France and met the employees that they would be working with: Alain, Paul, Michelle and Monique. Alain announced that he had made reservations for Wednesday evening at Willi's Wine Bar in Paris. "You need to have reservations for this place if you want to eat in the dining room. Although they do have a beautiful bar where you can eat."

"It sounds exciting. Of course everything about Paris sounds exciting to me. I have never been to a wine bar," said Sarah excitedly.

"This place has wonderful food," Michelle said.

They started off with a meeting with the engineers Monique and Michelle explaining to Sarah and Sam the problems they were having. For the first two days, Monday and Tuesday, they worked ten and twelve hours respectively. By Wednesday mid-afternoon the problem was solved so they finished with a meeting to make sure everyone understood what needed to be done. Sam and Sarah left the company around 4:00 P.M. and headed back to the hotel to get ready for their night out.

Alain and the others picked them up at the hotel at 7:00 pm as agreed upon and they took the train into Paris. *I just can't believe this. Who would have thought funny little Sarah Kincaid would be sitting on a train heading for Paris. Wait until I tell Daddy.*

As they entered Willi's Wine Bar Sarah was impressed with the long, polished oak bar and the exceptionally large selection of wines. They were led to the rear of the bar to their table. Sarah took her seat and immediately looked around to take everything in. She knew she was acting like a school kid, but she just never had exciting experiences like this as a child. The dining room had high oak beamed ceilings. Alain noticed that Sarah was staring at Willi's bottle art collection. "A new image from a different artist is added each year," he told Sarah.

"Everything is just wonderful, Alain. Thank you for bringing us."

"You're welcome," Alain said smiling. He was just realizing how naïve this beautiful young woman was. It was almost like she had just been set loose on the world. Paul thanked Sam and Sarah for their help. "We've been working on the problem for quite some time. It is just good now to finally be able to get on with other things," he said.

"When is your flight back home?" Monique asked.

"I tried to get us out tomorrow," answered Sam "but we can't get a flight until Friday morning."

"I thought, if it's okay with Alain," Monique continued with a pleading look at Alain, "that I would take the day off tomorrow and take Sarah around some of the shops."

"Sure, we've all spent a lot of overtime lately because of the problem. I think we all deserve a day off," was Alain's response.

"If you really mean that," piped up Michelle "I would like to take off Friday as my daughter has a little part in a play at school."

"Okay! What about you Paul?"

"Well, maybe I will take off tomorrow also and Sam and I can do some guy stuff then meet up with the girls for dinner."

"Now that is all settled, let's look at the menu," Alain said as he motioned the waiter over. Michelle noticed that Sam seemed to be having a difficult time reading the menu since it was in French.

"Do you want me to read the menu to you?" she asked Sarah and Sam.

"No, I have decided. I would like to have the roast lamb," Sarah said.

"Do you read French?" Paul asked.

"Yes. I speak and read it. My grandmother was French." She didn't do it to try to impress them. It just came naturally to her. Dinner was wonderful and after a cup of cappuccino they decided it was time to call it quits. Alain and Michelle said their goodbyes to Sam and Sarah, since they would not be seeing them again before they went back home. Alain shook Sam's hand, "Sam thank you again. It is always nice to see you," he said. "Sarah it was very nice to meet you. You helped so much and I hope that any time we have a problem and need some help that they will send you with Sam," he said. He felt himself wishing that *he* had offered to take off tomorrow and spend the time with Sam since they would be getting together with the two women for dinner. He was feeling he would like to spend more time with Sarah. He just enjoyed being around her. *She is so unique,* he thought.

Before going to bed Sarah called Tyler giving him her flight schedule and filling him in with her evening at Willi's Wine Bar and the wonderful food, and her plans for tomorrow.

Monique called for her just before noon. They took the train into Paris and then got on the Metro. "This is over one hundred years old," Monique informed her.

"Wow! I hope it is safe," she responded teasingly. They got off at Tuileries, Madeleine.

The beauty of this shopping area, which was called Place Vendome, impressed Sarah. It was so historical looking as compared to anything in Austin. She knew that *a city square* meant *place* in French. It was a large rectangle square which was surrounded by beautiful shops and the Ritz Hotel which once was an 18th century private residence; she had learned this information from Monique. There was a tall column with a statue on top in the middle of the square. She could tell just by looking around that these shops were out of her league. Her engineering salary, although not meager, was not enough for her to shop in them. They thought they would eat first and Monique knew of a little outdoor café where they could lunch without breaking the bank. *Sitting outside eating lunch is so Parisian.* Sarah thought. She enjoyed watching the people pass by. Some of the ladies had big bags from those expensive shops like, Cartier, Chanel, Piaget and Le Couturiers et Joailliers. "Who do you think these people are? Movie stars? Models? Perhaps the wives of big financiers?" Sarah inquired.

"Probably a mixture of all that. Of course many of them are tourists visiting from abroad. Probably a lot of Americans," Monique surmised.

They had fun just walking through the shops and window-shopping. Every shop they went in was so elegant. She wished she could buy something for Tyler. He was so laid back and casual that even if she could afford to buy, the clothes were all too fancy for him. Part of what she loved about him was that easy, laidback attitude. By the time they had said their goodbyes to Monique and Paul, Sarah was exhausted and was glad she had packed that morning. She took a bath and went to bed. *What a wonderful time this has been,* she thought, *but I will be so happy to see Tyler tomorrow night.*

Her plane arrived at 4:30 pm. Tyler was getting anxious waiting for it to arrive. It was half an hour late. When it finally arrived it seemed like an hour for the plane to taxi to the gate then another hour before the people started to exit the tunnel. Actually after the plane landed and Sarah exited the tunnel was about half an hour but not more than forty-five minutes. His heart leaped when he saw her. It had been less than a week but he felt it was much longer. They hugged and kissed.

"I don't have to ask you how France was?"

"It was wonderful Tyler. I really hope we can make a recreational trip there."

They picked up her luggage and by the time they got to the car it was about 6:00 pm. Once in the car he asked, "Have you had dinner?"

"No, but do you have something at home we can have? I really don't want to eat out. I just want to go home. I have had enough eating out."

"Well it isn't French but I have pasta leftover from last night. We can have it with a tossed salad and garlic bread. How is that?"

"That sounds great. I have missed coming home to you at night. Going back to a lonely hotel room was miserable."

Oh it is so good to have her back. I hope that she won't have to travel too much with her job, he thought.

CHAPTER 17

John asked Sarah and Sam to do a presentation of their findings at the plant in France for the higher up executives. Sarah and Sam worked together on the presentation and when they felt comfortable with what they had put together, John arranged for a meeting in the executives conference room. They would be presenting to the vice-president. It was the first time Sarah would present to the higher up executives and she was very nervous. On a normal day, Sarah wore pants. They freed her up to run back and forth from the lab to her office and she never worried about getting dirty. But on this day she decided to wear a suit. It was not a suit with pants, because Sarah didn't want them to think she was trying to be like one of the men. No, she chose to wear a suit with a skirt that came just below her knees, a tailored blouse and a pair of low heel pumps. She knew she was good at her job and that they all respected her work, so she wanted to make sure they were aware that she was a woman without being too sexy or trendy. She did this mostly for all the other women engineers. She worked very hard to try and represent them. She knew what it was like to be ignored in the engineering world because of being female. Although most of the managers were aware of the skills of many of the women engineers, some of them were still in the dark ages. Sarah wanted to remind them in any way she could without being verbal, that women were a great asset to the company.

The presentation went over extremely well. Sam had decided he would introduce the problem then let Sarah tell the attendees how they solved it. This would not only let her get her feet wet but it would let the executives see how knowledgeable she was in her job and how well versed she was. The vice-president congratulated Sarah and Sam on a job well done. John was extremely pleased as well, as it also made him look good. He was sure to let them know how much he appreciated them both. Later that day, John called Sarah into his office.

"Dr. Randolph was extremely impressed by your presentation. He said you were very clear and it flowed well," John said.

"Thank you. That makes me feel good. I knew that Sam and I put together a good presentation but I was nervous that I would not be able to communicate it well."

"Sarah, I'm putting in for a promotion for you," he said. "You know Steve Craig, one of our first line managers from Sam's Department, is moving to a different division?"

"Yes! I have heard that," she said holding her breath.

"I am nominating you for the job. Sam and I had a meeting about the position and we both agree that you are the right person for the job. You would then of course be reporting directly to Sam."

"Do you think I would fit in? I mean there are a few engineers who are vying for that position and will probably not be happy if I get it. They still look at me as a kid just out of school."

"I don't care what they think. I know your work and also how you work with your people."

"Thank you, John. I appreciate it very much."

"It still has to go through the upper echelon but after your presentation today, I don't think there will be a problem but you never know. I will keep you up-to-date."

Sarah was ecstatic. It wasn't just because of the title or the extra money, but rather it was more because of the acceptance of her work and another move forward for the women engineers. She called Tyler to tell him of her news. He was very happy and proud of her.

"Honey, tomorrow night I'm going to take you to one of the most upscale restaurants in Austin to celebrate."

"Well, I haven't gotten the job yet, but John is going to send his recommendation up to the next level. Oh honey, I think I have a good chance," she added excitedly.

"Well, we'll celebrate your nomination. How did the presentation go?"

"It went over really great, Tyler. Sam actually let me do all of the presenting. I must say, I was nervous but I didn't stumble once and just a little while ago John told me that Dr. Randolph, the vice-president, told him he was very impressed with me. Of course he knew it was the first time I've presented to the execs, so he may have added 'for a first-time presenter.'"

"Honey, you are good at what you do. Don't put yourself down. He meant what he said."

"Thanks Tyler. I will talk to you when I get home. I want to call my dad."

"Okay! 'Bye sweetie."

She called her father. "Baby, I'm so proud of you. I don't know where you got all the smarts from, but it surely wasn't from me."

"Daddy, will you be sure and tell momma?" She kept hoping that something she did would make her mother feel proud of her and admit she had made the right choice for her life.

"I will Sarah," he said knowing it wouldn't make any difference to Olivia.

"Sarah may be getting a promotion," John told his wife Olivia.

"Hm!" was all she could say. She had shown so much disapproval of Sarah that she didn't know how to be positive.

"I told her I was real proud of her. I support her in all she does because I trust her to do the right thing," Sarah's father said proudly.

"So do you think abandoning her parents was the right thing?" she asked huffily.

"Come on Liv, she didn't abandon us. Children graduate and move on with their own lives. You surely wouldn't want her wasting her life sitting around here and becoming an old maid. Sarah has lots of life inside her."

"Well let's hope she *doesn't* have life inside her. She's only been married a short while."

A month later Sarah got her promotion to First Line Manager. Some people were not happy that she had been promoted so soon, especially Jack Malone and Mike Johnson who had hoped that one of them would have got the promotion. They were the only two people in the

Disk Development area that did not congratulate her. She wasn't surprised.

Three days after returning from France, Sarah noticed the black car again. That night she mentioned it to Tyler.

"I can arrange my schedule tomorrow so that I can follow the car if it is there," he said

"I don't want to interrupt your schedule, Tyler. I know you have clients to take care of."

"I have a 5 o'clock meeting with Kevin I can change. He would be happy to do that. Can you leave around 5:30?"

"Yes! You know the door I come out of don't you?"

"The last one at the east side of the building?"

"Yes! Try and park close to it."

Tyler arrived at 5:20 pm. He was able to get into the parking lot since he had a contact inside. The guard called Sarah and she told him that it was okay to admit Tyler. After checking his identification the guard allowed him past. He found a parking spot near Sarah's car. He hadn't seen the black car outside but then he didn't quite know where to look. Ten minutes later Sarah exited the door. She walked to her car and noticed Tyler parked nearby. He watched her as she pulled out past the guard shack. About ten seconds later he saw the black car pull out of an area outside the shack. Tyler kept his distance from it but made sure he still had it and Sarah's car in sight. He thought it might be a Lexus It kept at least two cars behind Sarah's. Sarah entered the highway with the black car following, keeping his distance. Tyler also entered the highway. The turnoff to go to Tyler's ranch was about ten minutes once entering the highway. He saw Sarah's right signal blinking to turn off. She moved over to the right lane. The black car also moved over. There were no cars between Sarah's and it as they started to turn off and just one car between the black car and Tyler's, but both the driver of the black car and Tyler kept at a distance. Tyler signaled right and moved over. Suddenly the black car darted out of the right lane and back into traffic then sped on down the highway.

"He was definitely following you," Tyler said when they got home.

"Do you know it was a man?"

"No I never really saw him but why would a woman be following you? I didn't get close enough to read his license plate either."

"I would imagine that it's a man," she agreed.

"He must have been suspicious of me following him because as soon as I moved over to exit, he darted out, almost hitting another car. I couldn't get back out of my lane to follow him. I was hoping that after he got off of the freeway, I could get closer to him to get his license number."

"If he was speeding I wouldn't want you to follow him. If this happens again, promise me that you won't do that."

"I promise. I should call Detective Dan at the police station."

"Who is Detective Dan?"

"He is my Uncle Dan; my mother's brother, Dan Rogers. You met him at the wedding."

"Oh, that's right. I haven't seen him since. Well at least we could give him the information but I don't want him to do anything right now."

"Make sure you have your cell phone right beside you in the car. If this happens again, call me and let me know your location and we will figure out a safe place for you to wait for me."

"I feel so lucky to have you worry about me," she said wrapping her arms around his waist. "It makes me feel so special."

"Darlin' you *are* special."

Two weeks had passed and Sarah never saw the black car since that day when Tyler followed it. She believed that the driver had figured out that they were on to him and backed off; she hoped for good. However things did not get better for them.

Summer was starting to come to an end and Tyler decided it would be a good idea if they had an outdoor party before the cooler weather was upon them so they planned for it in two weeks. It would be small, mostly family. There would be his whole family, cousin Martha who asked if she could bring a friend and of course, Kevin and a date and Gloria, if she was in town. They would have a disc jockey, which Tyler would arrange for, and a buffet-style meal. Tyler and Sarah would prepare most of the meal.

"Dad says that he hopes you will prepare your famous quesadillas."

"For him, I will certainly make them."

"My parents are crazy about you."

"I'm glad! I love them too," she said then added a little sadly, "I wish my dad could come but I wouldn't want to invite him and not my mother. I know she won't come. Besides even if she would. I don't think I would enjoy myself, because I would feel like I was being scrutinized."

"Invite them both and if she doesn't come then it's your father's choice as to whether he comes or not. At least you will have invited them."

"Okay! That's a good idea. When I saw how much she seemed to enjoy herself at the wedding, I was hoping she was changing, but just when dad and I think that, she goes back to her old self."

They started preparing the food a few days early. They made chili that could easily be reheated on Saturday. Sarah decided she liked her salsa fresh so she would make it Saturday morning along with a tossed salad but the salad dressings could be made ahead of time. The quesadillas wouldn't take much time so she would do them on Saturday also. Tyler would barbeque chicken just prior to everyone coming. It wouldn't matter if it were still cooking when they arrived. They had bought shrimp and other finger foods at the deli. They were both quite excited. This would be their first party as a couple. Actually it was the first dinner party Tyler had thrown at his farm. Sarah went outdoors to make sure everything was okay. They had a gazebo that was large enough to let everyone dance and also a place for the disc jockey and the table with the food and bar. Tyler had it built for this purpose shortly after he got the house. He had wanted to entertain and now he was happy he had Sarah with him. He knew she would be the perfect hostess and he was so proud of her.

CHAPTER 18

On the night before the party Sarah noticed that Tyler was not very talkative. In fact he seemed quite distant.

"Was everything okay at work?"

"Yes!"

"Was everything okay with your day?"

"Yes!" he said rather irritated.

Sarah decided to leave him alone. Something certainly had happened but she didn't want to cause any more irritation. He frightened her. He had never acted this way with her before. He always looked lovingly at her and now he looked like he hated her.

That night he went to bed early and left her sitting watching television by herself. Again she decided she would leave him alone. Hopefully tomorrow he would feel better.

The next morning she got up and made coffee and left out some bagels. She was so disturbed by his behavior she couldn't eat. "Why is this happening?" she said aloud to herself. "Especially on the day of our party." She busied herself making the salsa and the salad. She had already made the dressings and she would make the quesadillas just before the guests arrived. At three o'clock the guests started to arrive. Her father had told her that it would be better if he didn't come. He said it would upset her mother. She told him that she understood and that she really didn't expect him to come. On top of everything else this also made her sad. She was having a lovely party but her parents wouldn't be there. Because of her mother's strange religion she was estranged from them. She especially felt bad because she knew her dad wanted to be a bigger part of her life. She hoped that once the party got going Tyler would forget whatever it was that was bothering him.

Cousin Martha came with a friend but it was a female friend. Everyone was a little surprised as they were hoping she had a date. Her name was Tanya. Sarah thought that if her tight top were any lower, her nipples would be showing. Also her skirt was so short Sarah just hoped she had underwear on. How rude to come to someone's party looking like that. After all, there were children there. Sarah noticed Tyler's mom giving Tanya a disapproving look. *She's probably thinking the same thing,* Sarah thought. One of the common ties they had was their strict religious upbringing, although Mrs. MacAulay's was conventional.

The food went over big and Mr. MacAulay kept telling Sarah that she made the best quesadillas in town. He was enjoying himself and had got Sarah up to dance a few times, but not Tyler. Not even when *The Keeper of the Stars* was being played. She always thought of this song as theirs. The disc jockey was good and played a mixture of classic rock, oldies and country. Tyler seemed to be enjoying himself all right. In fact she thought he had a little too much to drink and the party had only been going on for a few hours. She also noticed that Tanya was flirting outrageously with him. Sarah hated the way she was feeling. She knew it was jealousy. By the time another hour went by, Tanya and Tyler were on the dance floor and she was rubbing her body all over him. What made her angry was that Tyler was not moving away from her. *Why is he doing this? What did I do? This is not like Tyler,* she thought.

Alice MacAulay was watching them disapprovingly. She knew that Sarah was terribly distraught. She wanted to knock that woman Tanya's head off. Alice loved Sarah like her own daughter.

"What is going on with Tyler and Sarah?" Conor asked Kevin.

"I'm not sure but I feel like going over and knocking my buddy to the floor," Kevin said feeling bad for his cousin.

"I'll help you. Maybe I should just tell cousin Martha to leave and take her slutty friend with her," Conor said.

"Well I don't suppose it is our place but I'm sure going to give Tyler a good tongue lashing for treating Sarah this way," Kevin said.

Sarah knew Kevin and Conor were talking about Tyler's behavior and she saw the looks Mrs. MacAulay was giving him. She did not know how to handle the situation so she turned and ran back to the house. She not only was feeling jealous but she felt humiliated in front of everyone.

Alice saw Sarah run to the house. She didn't want to make a scene with Tyler but she wanted to somehow let him know that Sarah was upset with him and had left the party.

"I wish that little slut would leave him alone for even a moment," she said in a whisper.

"What?" Ian MacAulay said turning his head towards his wife.

"Nothing dear. I'm just trying to get Tyler's attention."

"Well, for crying out loud that's easy. Hey Tyler. Come here a minute," he yelled. "Your mom wants to talk to you."

She was annoyed at him. "I was trying not to bring too much attention to the situation."

Tyler walked a little unsteadily towards his mother. She wasn't used to seeing him drink. Whatever amount of beer he had was more than he could handle. His eyes were a little droopy and he had a grin on his face. "Hey mom! What's up?"

"Walk with me a little ways." Once they were away from earshot of everyone she asked, "What is going on between you and Sarah?"

His grin faded. "Why?"

"Because she watched you and that girl behaving so badly and she left the party. It was a disgusting scene."

He hesitated a moment and looked around as if looking for her. "Where did she go?"

"Towards the house," she answered "and I hope you straighten this out. We are all upset with you for the way you have humiliated her."

Tyler had known there was going to be a show-down but he hoped it would have happened after the party. He knew he shouldn't have acted the way he did but he was mad. He walked into the hallway towards the kitchen when she came out of their bedroom. Her face was wet with tears and her eyes were red. He had never seen her cry before and it broke his heart, but she had already broken it. She walked into the kitchen and just stood staring at him. Suddenly he saw Sarah as he had never seen her before. Her green eyes blazed with anger. "What are you trying to do to me? Did it make you feel good to make me feel jealous and humiliated? Today was supposed to be a happy day. I worked just as hard as you did to make it happy," she said banging her fist on the counter. "But what was my reward? My husband behaving inappropriately with someone he just met," she was yelling and crying. He had never heard her raise her voice like that nor did he think she had it in her to show so much anger. He was stunned into silence. He stared at her with his mouth open.

Lowering her voice she said, "I have never felt this way before and I hate it."

Finally getting his voice he said, "Do you want to talk of jealousy?" he walked over to the desk drawer and took out a manila folder and threw it on the table. She walked to the table and took a picture out of the folder. She stared at it for a while then looked straight at him.

"What is this supposed to mean?"

"Isn't it obvious? This is you and Sam all dressed up, obviously going into a hotel room."

"You put me through all this because of this photo?" she asked angrily.

"Is it supposed to be okay for you and Sam to be going into a hotel room together? You told me you would never go to each other's rooms."

"Tyler, this was at the electronic show I attended in Las Vegas a month ago. Because the company wanted all the employees to get to know each other, because we were from different offices and different states . . ."

"Oh so they wanted you to go to a hotel room with another employee?" he interrupted.

"No, it was a hospitality suite. There was a small party going on in there for all the employees that went to the show."

A door opened "So there you are! I was wondering what happened to you." Sarah was furious that this woman could be so bold as to walk into their home.

"The party is outdoors," she said with her eyes as icy as her voice.

"I wasn't talking to you," Tanya said in a disrespectful voice.

This further infuriated Sarah and her voice became angrier, "I know who you were talking to but the party is still outdoors and you are intruding upon *our* private moment in *our* private home. Please close the door on your way out."

"Tyler?" Tanya was hoping that he would come to her defense.

"She's right! The party *is* outdoors," he said without turning to look at her. He was staring at Sarah. Tanya felt the resentment but thought she would push her luck a little more.

"When will you be back out?"

"*We* will be out when *we* are through" Sarah said very sternly.

Tanya gave some little annoying sound and turned and walked back out.

Tyler felt foolish. "You mean there was a party going on inside that room?"

"Yes, that's exactly what was going on."

She looked away and tried to relax. She rolled her head. She was tired and stressed. This had all been a strain on her.

"Why didn't you bring this to me when you first got it? And by the way when and how did you get it? I don't even remember it being taken."

"It was mailed to me. No return address. I received it yesterday and I didn't want to deal with it before the party."

"No, you didn't want to spoil the party for you but you sure spoiled it for me. This was the most awful day of my life."

"I'm sorry Sarah. I can't bear the thought of you with someone else."

She looked back at the picture. *Where are the other people?* she thought.

"This has been digitally changed. There were two other people with us."

"What do you mean?"

"With a program like Photoshop you can remove objects or people or add things. You can make all kinds of changes."

"I'm not familiar with Photoshop. What are you suggesting?"

"Tyler, if you would have shown this to me last night, I could have explained it very easily. I would not have had to suffer all of the anger and humiliation I felt today," her voice was getting louder and angry again. "You could have ruined our relationship."

"My heart sank when I saw it. I couldn't talk about it last night. I was really down."

All of a sudden she had that insecure little girl look. "Tyler, this not only hurts me but it makes me very sad because you don't love me as much as I thought you did."

"Of course I do. That is why I felt so bummed out when I saw the picture."

"If you loved me the way I thought you did, you would have realized there must be an explanation and came and asked me about it. Instead you looked at the picture and decided I was cheating on you, and committing adultery with a man whose wife I consider a friend. You also judged me as a liar." She turned her back on him and walked towards the window. The tears started to flow again. "What did I do to make you think you couldn't trust me?"

He walked over to her and turned her around to face him. He had tears in his eyes also. "Baby, you are flawless. You have never done anything wrong. I am just a stupid, immature fool who doesn't deserve you and who is afraid of not being able to hold on to you."

"Tyler if one of us is suspicious of the other, we have to bring it to the table immediately. You interpreted that picture wrong and caused a terrible day for me. I don't ever want to feel like this again. My life with you before this had been like heaven but this whole experience was hell."

"Sarah, I'm sorry," he said wiping her tears with a tissue.

"I am glad Daddy wasn't here to see that. He probably would have knocked you out."

"I wouldn't blame him. I don't know how to make it all go away but if you come out with me now I promise I will be by your side the rest of the day and I will not drink anymore. I can't handle anymore anyway. I already have a headache."

"Okay, but if you as much as look at that little tramp, *I* will knock you out."

"I won't do anything. Maybe I'll tell my cousin to take her home."

"Let me go wash my face."

They went back out to the party. Tanya was not happy to see Tyler's arm around Sarah's waist. He walked over to the Disc Jockey then walked back to Sarah. He led her out on the dance floor as *Keeper of the Stars* was playing. Mrs. MacAulay started clapping and everyone joined in. Tyler smiled at Sarah; he knew she was feeling embarrassed, but she smiled back. Everyone was relieved to see them together, except for Tanya. She attempted to approach him but he never left Sarah's side. Tanya was hoping to have lured Tyler away from Sarah. She had had her eye on him five years ago when he graduated with her brother's class from college but then he moved away. Now that he was back she was determined to get him for herself but this woman Sarah had gotten in the way. Mrs. MacAulay took the opportunity when Martha walked over to the food table to talk to her.

"Martha dear, I think it would be a good idea to take your friend home. She has caused a terrible scene here."

"I'm sorry Aunt Alice. I'm terribly embarrassed about her behavior. We will leave." She kissed her aunt and walked over to Tyler and Sarah and apologized.

"If I would have thought she was going to act like that, believe me I would never have brought her. She almost begged me to bring her." Sarah reached over and gave Martha a hug.

"We know it was not your fault." She said goodbye to them then walked over to the table where Tanya was, picked up her purse and said, "Come on Tanya, we are leaving."

"Oh, Martha let's not go yet," she pleaded with her.

"We have been asked to leave." Tanya was angry.

Sarah was happy to see her go. "We'll make sure Martha doesn't bring her back."

Tyler smiled "I think she would be afraid to face you again. You shocked me they way you talked to her. You were tough."

"I hated her audacity and her disrespect of me. I was her host also. She walks right in with her breasts hanging out and flirts outrageously with you. I have my pride. I won't let a floozy like that treat me the way she did," she said still feeling angry with Tanya.

"I can't apologize enough, honey. I caused the whole thing. I was in a rotten mood and I drank too much. I hated the way she treated you too. It won't happen again" he said hugging her.

His family said their goodbyes. "It was a great party, Tyler," his father said.

"It could have been better," his mother said in a rather loud voice. As she was hugging Tyler she said in a whisper, "don't you ever treat my little girl like that again or I will give you a showing up in front of everybody. "

"Yes ma'am!" Tyler said smiling at his mom. He was happy that she loved Sarah so much, especially since she didn't get much love and attention from her own mom.

"Kevin and I almost went over and knocked your head off," said Conor. "Everyone was so ticked off at you. I kept thinking 'what is the matter with him. He's making out with a floozy when he has that beautiful girl over there,'" he said shaking his head as though he couldn't believe his brother's behavior.

"There was a misunderstanding on my part between Sarah and me. It wasn't that I thought the other girl was hotter than Sarah. In my eyes, nobody is. I'm sorry I messed up the party for everyone."

Conor slapped him on the upper arm "No, we all enjoyed it, but the best part was when both of you made up and came out and danced."

After everyone left Tyler took her in his arms and said, "Let's make up for last night."

"Just promise me that this was a learning experience," she said.

"It definitely was. I have never felt so stupid and then to have a little girl like you set me straight."

"Well now you have seen my *other* side. I hope you still love me," she said teasingly.

"Of course I do. I was very impressed by you."

"I wasn't trying to impress you, Tyler, but I don't want us to break up because of jealousy and misinterpretation or lies. We have to be honest and up front with each other because there are people and situations that could break us up and it would kill me."

He leaned over her and smiled gently into her face "I really did learn my lesson, babe, thanks to you."

"Okay, I believe that Tanya didn't mean anything to you and what happened with you and her was because of the picture." She put her head on his shoulder and he kissed her head.

"Baby, Tanya is at the other end of the spectrum from you. She is definitely not my type."

"I hope not because I wouldn't like to think I fit into her category."

"No way! I'm tired. Let's go to bed before I get more tired." He stood up and helped her to her feet then to her surprise he picked her up and carried her to the bedroom. He laid her on the bed and leaning over her he looked into her eyes and said, "Whenever we have a bad day that threatens our relationship and we get it straightened out, I am going to carry you over the threshold of our bedroom and start again, putting the bad time behind us. In other words it is forgotten and we move on. Do you agree?"

"I agree as long as the bad day doesn't repeat itself. In other words, we have to learn from each *bad day.*"

"Agreed," he smiled and kissed her. "You're amazing. One moment you're like a little girl who is so helpless and in the next you're like this wise old woman."

"I had a lot of time on my hands growing up" she smiled.

CHAPTER 19

Olivia Kincaid stood in her daughter's room for the first time since Sarah left home to go to college. The few times that she had come home Sarah washed her own sheets and made the bed before she went back to Austin so her mom wouldn't feel the need to go to the room. Olivia had been feeling more and more hopeless and helpless. Her world had been centered on her daughter and she thought by raising her in the church, Sarah would always be with her. She thought Sarah would have gotten as involved as she had. It was harder for her than either her husband or daughter imagined. Olivia had never been able to show her real feelings so that hurt usually came out as anger or disapproval. She stood looking around remembering when she would come up and tuck Sarah in bed and share some wise thoughts from Reverend Barker's sermon. She walked over and touched the sheets and blanket that she used to tuck in then pulled the duvet as though pulling it over Sarah to make sure she wouldn't be cold. She looked at a picture of Sarah when she was six years old with her daddy. Oh how she longed for that little girl.

She walked over to the closet expecting to see the clothes that Sarah had left behind. The ones she was made to wear when she lived there. She was surprised to see that it was empty. *Why would Sarah take the clothes with her?* she thought. *Maybe she took them to the Salvation Army.*

She walked over to the window seat where Sarah often sat and did her homework. It was also a storage chest. She lifted the lid and there they were, all neatly folded. Olivia couldn't help thinking how much the chest reminded her of a coffin with Sarah's past buried in it. *Was that what Sarah was intending, to bury her past?* she thought sadly. *Was her life here really that miserable? Was Sarah unable to share her true feelings also or was it just with me, her mother?* Olivia's thoughts were interrupted when her husband walked in.

"Livia, you haven't been in Sarah's room since she left. Is everything okay?"

"I found Sarah's old clothes buried in this coffin," she said almost absent-mindedly.

"It's just a storage chest," John said watching her with concern. "She probably left them for you to decide what to do with them. Perhaps you can give them to the church for some other young girl to wear," John suggested.

"I don't think so. Every time I would see a young girl in Sarah's clothes it would just remind me of the time when I had Sarah by my side."

John patted her back saying, "I'm going to take Tweed for a walk," and then he walked out the door.

Olivia knew her husband had a lady friend. She never said anything because she knew if she was to complain and he gave up being friends with Kathleen, then she would be expected to be more of a companion to him. Olivia didn't know how to communicate with her husband but she had a certain amount of love and respect for him. Even though the church tried to encourage her to leave John, she couldn't. He was kind and took care of her and Sarah. He had asked her to go to marriage counseling a couple of times, but she refused. She wouldn't be able to sit and talk to a stranger about her personal life. She wished things had been different. She wished she had been different. *Now John is comforted by Kathleen and Tyler comforts Sarah.* She was alone. Maybe she could find it inside herself to let go and show her love to her daughter. She was afraid if she did it would look like she was accepting the lifestyle. *Maybe it wasn't so much Sarah's lifestyle,* Olivia thought, *maybe it's because she is so beautiful and innocent. Maybe I am really afraid for my daughter. After all, I don't want what happened to me to happen to my daughter. Rape is an unforgiving crime.*

John Kincaid walked his border collie Tweed to the park. He sat down on a bench and started throwing a Frisbee for Tweed to retrieve. He thought about Olivia and how that had been a big step for her to go to Sarah's room. Perhaps she could tear down the wall and accept Sarah's new life. *That would be wonderful,* he thought. He knew he could have left Olivia but in some odd way he still loved her. Maybe it was more pity. She had no one to love her. He also knew that she couldn't take care of herself financially unless she cleaned other people's homes. She was extremely good at housekeeping and cooking. Olivia needed someone to take care of. To her that was her job, just like Tweed thought his job was to retrieve the Frisbee. He bought Tweed thinking that maybe a little dog could be her friend and she could take care of it but she showed no interest in the dog. John on the other hand, loved Tweed. He was such a companion to him when he was not with Kathleen. John decided he would drive to Austin next weekend and get to know Tyler's family a bit better. He was feeling a need to be more a part of Sarah's life. He needed her and couldn't seem to bring Olivia around to be part of her life also. It didn't seem like there was anything he could do for his wife. The only thing that would seem to make her happy would be to have Sarah home and he certainly did not want that for his little girl. She was happy and he would never allow anyone to take that away from her.

CHAPTER 20

John had called and made arrangements with his daughter to come and visit. Sarah and Tyler planned that on Saturday when her father arrived they would spend it alone so that he and Tyler could get to know one another a lot better. On Sunday they would invite Tyler's parents over for a buffet lunch so they could get together with Sarah's father before he drove back to Marshallville.

It was a very happy time for Sarah. On Saturday, as planned, all three of them went riding out to the lake. John had never felt so much peace as he did at this moment. He was on a beautiful mare with a wonderful disposition; he had a picnic with his daughter and her husband at their private lake; but most of all he was with his ecstatically happy, liberated daughter. It almost made him cry to see how much in love she was and how at peace she was with her life. *I could die at this moment and be content,* he thought. *What more could a father ask for than his child grow up healthy and happy?*

That evening they went to the Irish Pub and met with Kevin. It was such a fun evening. Kevin and John had never had such a good time together. "You and my dad ought to come down some time together and spend more time here with us. They have a dart board here and a couple of pool tables in the back."

"You know Kevin," said John "that's a good idea. My brother and I don't spend enough time together and now that we have a place to get away from everything, this is perfect."

"Even if it was just one weekend a month," Tyler piped in "it would be great for everyone, especially for the Kincaids since you don't get together often. My family gets together all the time."

By the time John got up, showered and went downstairs, Sarah had coffee waiting for him. He was looking forward to seeing Ian and Alice today. He got his mug of coffee and went out to see the horses with Tweed and Lady. He really loved being at the farm. The MacAulays arrived around one o'clock in the afternoon.

"How do you do John," said Ian, reaching his hand. "It's good to see you again."

"It's good to see you too, Ian."

"Was Olivia not able to come down this time?" Alice asked. "We do hope to see her again soon. She did such a wonderful job raising Sarah. We just love her to pieces."

"Thank you. I will let her know you approve," he said smiling. He liked Mrs. MacAulay. She was kind and had a bubbly personality. She was always fussing around making sure everybody had what he or she needed.

Sarah thought that was such a lovely thing Mrs. MacAulay said to her dad and she was sure he would tell her mother. The MacAulays only spent a little more than three hours at the farm because they knew John had to drive home, but it was a delightful three hours and they had gotten to know each other a lot more.

When John left he let Sarah know what a wonderful time he had and how much he respected Tyler and his family. "I couldn't ask for anyone better for my little girl and I can see how his parents love you and have welcomed you. That makes me very happy." Once again he apologized for her mom. "You know Sarah, I really think she would like to come and see you but she just doesn't know how to let go of her emotions. She does love you, even if she doesn't show it."

"I know Dad, but I don't know how to reach her. Tell her I send my regards and that I love her, and Daddy please come back soon."

"I intend to come back often Sarah. This was a very liberating experience for me and I intend to talk to my brother about coming with me. You know, Andrew likes to ride also."

"Kevin and I thought we would arrange for you both to come soon."

At that moment Tyler walked in and shook John's hand and invited him to come back as often as he liked. "It brightens Sarah up to have you be a part of us all."

"Thank you, Tyler. As I told Sarah, I intend to come back often. I enjoy being here and being with your family."

John made sure he told Olivia what Alice MacAulay said of her raising such a wonderful girl. It actually brought a look of surprise to her eyes. "That was nice of her. No one has ever said that to me and I do take it as a huge compliment," Olivia said to John's surprise. John made a point to share Olivia's response with Sarah.

CHAPTER 21

A few more weeks had passed and Sarah still hadn't seen the black car. She started getting notes in the mail at home, however. Tyler was already home and had picked up the mail when Sarah got there. He handed her a piece of mail that had no return address. Without saying anything he watched her as she opened it. She had a disturbed, confused look on her face.

"What is it?" Tyler inquired.

"Nothing. Junk mail," she said crushing the note in her hand and throwing it in the waste bin.

However, Tyler noticed a little while later that the note was not in the waste bin anymore even though the bin had not been emptied. He decided not to make a big deal out of it but it did concern him.

A few days later, Tyler picked up the mail and noticed another piece of mail for Sarah with no return address. He thought about opening it. After all if it were just junk mail, why would she care? While contemplating opening the envelope, the phone rang.

"Hello!" Tyler said into the phone. He waited but there was no answer. The person was still on the other end of the phone. "Hello!" Tyler said again. Click! The caller hung up. Sarah came home and Tyler mentioned it to her but she just shrugged her shoulders. She had brought home some Chinese take-out and started to set it out on the table. Tyler walked over to the mail to give her the mystery mail but it was gone. She had already picked it up.

For the next couple of weeks the mysterious mail came and Tyler had picked up the phone several times from the phantom caller. He had asked Sarah about the mail and she said it was just some company trying to give her a credit card. He tried to accept that answer but he felt uneasy about all of it. It was affecting their relationship. Even while making love to her, he felt somehow that she was keeping something from him. Something or some-one was coming between them. He was so uncomfortable that on her next trip to France, he booked a flight the day after hers and a return flight the day before she was due to return. He hated himself for doing it but he loved Sarah so much he couldn't let anything or anyone get between them. He knew it wasn't Sam. He had met Sam and his wife and could see the loyalty in their relationship and the pride they had in their two children. But if there were someone else, this would be a perfect opportunity for Sarah and him to get together.

He watched her and Sam get into their rented car and drive to Carp, Inc. of France. Except for taking some time for lunch, he sat in his car making sure Sarah didn't leave. She too, left for lunch but always with some of the co-workers and he watched them as they came back. Around five o'clock, she and Sam would get into the car and drive back to the hotel. After three days he was con-vinced nothing was going on and returned home a day sooner than planned.

When Tyler got home he picked up the mail and started to sort it out. There were a couple more of those letters. Sarah had said it was an offer for a credit card but he was suspicious of the fact that there was no company name on the envelope or advertising of the low interest rate they were offering. It was just a plain envelope. Once again he was tempted to open it but decided to put it in her desk. When he opened the desk drawer, he was surprised to see the other plain envelopes. They were open so he began to read them. "Hello Sarah! Do not worry, pretty soon you will be in Heaven; Hello Sarah! I will take care of everything; Hello Sarah! Your worries will soon be over." Tyler couldn't read anymore. He felt sick in his stomach. Who was this person and what was Sarah telling him? What worries? What was he going to take care of?

For the next two days, Tyler got angrier and angrier. At first he was angry with this unknown person, then with Sarah. She had lied to him about the notes. Were there other things she had lied about? Did she know who the phantom caller was? Was she having an affair? She had told him that she was in heaven just being with him. Was she lying about that? Did she even love him?

By the time he picked Sarah up at the airport, he was so angry and confused he couldn't speak to her. She had bounded into his arms but he didn't put them around her. Of course she knew something was terribly wrong.

"Darling, what is it?" she asked.

"Sarah, let's just get your luggage and go home. We'll talk then," he said.

"Okay!" Sarah said submissively. The drive home was unbearable. Tyler didn't say a word and Sarah had to keep from asking him to tell her what was wrong. She kept looking at him for signs but there was nothing. She was terrified. He was at least a hundred times more distant from her now than he had been the night he came home with the photograph. They had been separated for almost a week and he couldn't even bear to put his arms around her.

When they got home, he got her luggage and opened the front door. He stood back to let her in. At least he was still polite to her. That was Tyler, always the gentleman. Even if he hated her, he would always be polite to her. He left the luggage in the entry hall and walked into her office. She started to follow him in but he came out and walked into the kitchen. He threw the letters on the table.

"Okay! I have brought the problem to the table. Just as you requested."

She gazed down at the plain envelopes. She had told him that their relationship should be based on honesty and she had lied to him. She didn't know how to explain why she had lied. The reason sounded ridiculous but the truth was, she didn't want him to be any more worried about her than he already was. She wanted to cry.

She looked up at him and he could see the fear in her eyes. "I am sorry I lied to you about these, but I really can explain."

"I hope you can Sarah, because for the past few days I have been wondering what else you have lied about," he said trying not to feel sorry for her.

"Nothing, Tyler. I haven't lied about anything else. I just didn't want you to worry again. Now that the black car has stopped following me, I didn't want you to worry about this."

"Why should I be worrying about you? I believe I should be worrying about me. After all, the notes aren't exactly threatening you. Someone is offering you heaven;

promising to take away all your worries; promising to take care of everything for you. Am I your worries, Sarah?"

"Tyler, no! Please believe me. I don't know who wrote these notes or why." She was crying by now.

"I suppose you don't know who has been making the calls either?" he said sarcastically, even though he was tempted to take her in his arms and comfort her.

"I don't know who made the calls."

"Sarah, this is all hard for me to believe. If it is the same person that made the crank calls to the agency; who followed you in the car from your work; who sent these notes and made the phone calls to our home, then he knows an awful lot about you and I am not the one giving him the information."

She was at a loss for words. This was her mistake and she didn't know how to correct it. How could she convince him that she hadn't done anything to hurt him, except lie about those stupid notes? She just stood staring at him with tears in her eyes and a confused look on her face. It was that little girl look that always melted his heart. He was determined this time it wouldn't work.

"I don't even know that you're not acting when you put that look on your face."

She looked down immediately not wanting him to have to look at her face. Things were going from bad to worse. *Now he doesn't believe my pain,* she thought.

"Sarah, at least look at me while I am talking to you."

By this time she was trembling. He was angry when she looked at him and he was angry when she looked away. She looked back at him and he couldn't stand it. He turned his head from her. Sarah ran into the bedroom and locked the door. Tyler stood in the middle of the kitchen floor and sighed. He knew he hadn't handled this well. He was totally confused. He wasn't sure he knew this woman that he loved so much. A big part of him believed her but he wanted to make sure she was being honest. He always said she didn't seem real; that she was too good to be true. He decided it was time to leave it for now and go to bed.

"Sarah, unlock this door. I want to go to bed and this *is* my bedroom," he said tiredly.

The door opened. "Yes, it is *your* bedroom, Tyler," she said as she walked out.

Once again Tyler sighed. He started to walk out after her but decided to get out of his suit and change into casual clothes. When he walked into the living room all the lights were out. He turned on the switch.

"Please turn off the light. I don't want you to look at me." He turned off the light and she felt him sit on the couch beside her.

"When I left Marshallville I felt so free. I was leaving the place of rejection; the place of humiliation; the place of loneliness; the place of hurt and pain; the place where the only love I felt was from my father." She hesitated then added, "Right now, Marshallville seems like a safe place. I want to just sit here in the dark and retreat to that safe place. I don't want anyone to look at me," she said with such hurt and confusion in her voice. Tyler felt pain that he had never felt before. This was his Sarah. Sarah the engineer that talked with such knowledge; Sarah the model that walked and smiled with such confidence; Sarah the hostess that made everyone so comfortable; Sarah the lover that loved him in a way nobody else had ever done. He was always amazed at how confident she always seemed to be but every once in a while he would catch Sarah, the insecure little girl. This was the Sarah that was sitting next to him now. He had reached that vulnerable spot in her and the little girl came out more than she had ever done before. His heart felt heavy and there was a lump in his throat so big he knew if he tried to talk he would cry. He wanted to cry. He wanted to cry for Sarah. He wanted to hold her but was unsure if that was the right thing to do right now. She seemed to indicate that she wanted to be alone.

"Sarah, what would you like me to do for you right now?" he said with such compassion.

"I want you to believe me. I really am not a liar, Tyler. I did want to protect you from worrying about me anymore than you already have. I have to be honest with you; I am really scared of this person. I don't know who he is and why he has zeroed in on me. I just want it to stop. I want the chance to just be happy with you."

"I believe you, baby. When I saw those letters I was so hurt. I thought you were having an affair. I thought that you had fallen out of love with me," he hesitated then added "Sarah, I even followed you to France and stalked you. I watched you get in the car with Sam and followed you to the place where you worked. I sat out there all day and watched you go to lunch with your co-workers and waited until you and Sam left for the day. I sat in my car outside your hotel until nine or ten o'clock at night."

"Oh Tyler, sometimes I think we love one another too much."

"I'm the one that always seems to cause our problems. Maybe I'm just too jealous."

"No, darling, this whole thing has been so bizarre. I would feel the same way if the tables were turned," she confessed.

"Someone is screwing around with us. He's trying to separate us. He's been following you. He is trying to get you to himself. We need to find out who this creep is. I'll talk to Uncle Dan again."

CHAPTER 22

Tyler and Sarah decided to ignore the letters and phone calls but they kept coming. It was causing such stress between them that Sarah decided to move out. At least Tyler wouldn't have to be involved with the phone calls and the letters. She moved while Tyler was at work. She left him a note telling him to contact her on her cell phone when he needed. Tyler called her immediately but she didn't answer. He was beside himself. Why would she put herself in such danger and not let him know where she was? He knew she was trying to protect him. Her moving out was not going to help him in any way. He would constantly be worrying about her. Not knowing was worse. She may have thought she would be protecting him but he wanted to protect her. She was the one in danger.

It had been a few days since she left and he hadn't heard from her. He tried her cell phone but she had it turned off. He knew Kevin hadn't heard from her but he called him anyway.

"Kevin, I would like to find out if Sarah's dad has heard from her but I don't want to worry him. Can you think of a way that you might be able to find out?"

"Well I do call him on occasion but I don't know how to ask without letting him know she has moved out. I mean you are my friend and business partner and she is supposed to be with you. He would surely know something was wrong if I asked," Kevin replied.

"Maybe your sister could call him to get Sarah's number and see what happens," suggested Tyler.

"That's an idea. He wouldn't suspect anything," Kevin agreed. After hanging up the phone it rang.

"Tyler, I'm sorry I haven't called you before this. It was totally selfish of me. I have been so disturbed about what is happening . . ."

"Sarah," he interrupted. "I have been worried sick about you. I want you to come home."

"I'm going home to visit my parents for a few days. I need to talk with my dad. I will talk to you when I get back. We need to figure how to not let this person control our lives if we are to stay together."

"Okay babe, we'll talk. Call me as soon as you get back."

Her mother was happy to see her. She hadn't come home by herself for a long time. She spent the afternoon with her mother and for the first time Olivia didn't seem to be so obsessed with Sarah's appearance. They baked bread. John always liked his wife's homemade bread. He came home a little early since he knew Sarah was there. They had dinner and sitting around the table with her parents gave Sarah a sense of safety. Like she was a little girl again and this awful thing was not happening. After she and her mother had finished cleaning up in the kitchen, they went into the living room and joined her dad.

"I want to ask you both not to tell anyone I am here. Even though it is only for a couple of days. Whoever has been following me and sending those crazy notes always seems to know my moves."

"Sarah, we haven't been talking to people about your whereabouts," her mother said almost defensively.

"I mean anyone, even Reverend Barker. Mom I don't want you to tell him anything about me. I know you tell him things because you said he keeps me in his prayers."

"He is concerned for you. After all, he was your pastor all during your growing up years."

"Olivia, I know what Sarah is saying. This person seems to know her comings and goings and if she is going to be able to stop him from having so much knowledge, everyone in her life has to keep her whereabouts almost a secret until we find out what is going on. You have my word, dear. I will not say anything other than you are doing fine," her dad said and looked at Olivia like he was forcing her to agree.

"Well, I surely don't want anything to happen to you, so I will do as you say," her mother agreed.

After a few days, Sarah announced that she was going back to Austin. "I was hoping you wouldn't have to go so soon. I thought you were having a good time," her mom said.

"I did have a good time, Momma and we will have some more good times."

As they were saying their goodbyes, Olivia actually moved towards Sarah and hugged her. It took Sarah, and her dad by surprise.

Driving home, Sarah kept the image of her mom hugging her, in the front of her mind. She was trying to understand what her mom was feeling. The hug almost felt desperate.

Alice MacAulay called her brother Dan at the police station. "Dan do you have any clues as to who is stalking Sarah? We are all at our wits end over this. Now she has moved out and is on her own and none of us know where she is," Alice said sounding very stressed.

"Why did she do that?" Dan asked angrily.

"I think she is trying to protect Tyler from all this. His business has suffered a little because of it."

"Well she is going to have to let *me* know where she is if she wants protection. I will call her on her cell phone," Dan said concerned. However he was not able to get a hold of her but he left a message telling her that he was angry with her for putting herself in danger and that if she didn't call him back with her new home phone number and address that he could no longer give her protection.

It had been a week since she left Tyler. She called him the day that she got home from her parent's house. "Hi Tyler! Just want you to know I'm back."

"How did things go?" he asked her.

"Actually quite well. Mom was happy to have me and she never complained about the way I look and dress. It was quite nice. I was afraid she was thinking I was home for good. She was not very happy when I left. She was different Tyler. She actually hugged me. There was no more of the 'no nonsense attitude.'"

"I'm happy for you, darling. When are you coming home?"

"Let me call you in a few days. I am just trying to get this guy off my trail."

"Well you better call Detective Dan. He is not happy with you for moving out and not getting in touch with him."

"I know. Let him know I will get to him in a few days."

"No Sarah! You call him now."

"Okay, I will call him." She knew he was going to be angry with her but she knew she should call anyway. She had told Tyler she would.

"Uncle Dan, it's Sarah . . ."

"Sarah, if you want our protection, you don't take yourself out from under it."

"I'm sorry. Things just got so bad for Tyler and me. Not anything between ourselves, just the stress of this outsider wedging between us."

"Well, I want you to check in with me every day, regardless of what is going on. I would rather you move back home."

"I know you would. I will check in. I promise."

CHAPTER 23

She entered through a different gate and parked in the parking lot on the north end. Going into the door at the north entrance she walked the length of the building down to the southeast part where she worked. She had been doing this for a few weeks now. She managed to get through her business but John knew she was very distressed.

"Sarah, Sam has been keeping me abreast with what's been going on. Take off as much time as you require. You have enough on your mind without all this work," John suggested.

"I appreciate your concern, John, but I can cope. Really."

"Okay! I will leave it to your own judgment but just know Sam and I understand."

"Thanks John. I will certainly let you know if I'm having trouble with the job."

He left and she went back to her work. She was feeling very lonely however and decided to call Gloria and see if they could get together.

"Hey Gloria! How are you?"

"Sarah, it is so good to hear from you. What are you up to?"

"Not much. I am feeling a little lonely. Do you think we can get together sometime and just talk?"

"What are you doing tonight?"

"Nothing. Can we get together?"

"Girlfriend, why don't you come to my place instead of us going out? That way we can have privacy. I assume you are calling from work, so why don't you come straight here and we will have something to eat?"

"Thanks, Gloria. I will be there around 6 o'clock. Is that okay?"

"Sure honey, I'll see you then."

He was able to get past the guard shack because he had a badge which he stole from a male employee, Bill Collins, in a bar restroom several weeks ago. He was aware that a group of men from the company stopped by this particular bar every Friday after work for a few beers. He watched and waited for the opportunity to present itself. It wasn't too long before Collins made the mistake he was waiting for. He followed the employee into the bathroom. After Collins relieved himself he walked over to the sink to wash his hands. He took his badge off from around his neck to splash his face with some cold water. By the time Collins dried off his face with paper towels, his badge was gone.

He had stayed away from Carp for a few weeks because he knew that Collins would have let security know that his badge had been stolen. Security personnel at the guard shacks would be checking badges very carefully to make sure the picture matched the person carrying it. Of course the badge would be deactivated immediately so that it would not be useful in getting into any of the buildings. Not that he cared. He just wanted to be able to get past the security guard and into the parking lot. For the past couple of days he had waited but she had not come out of this gate. He didn't know she had taken almost a week off. He thought perhaps she was trying to throw him off by parking in a different area and entering and leaving by a different gate.

He arrived in the parking lot early to cruise around to see if she was using another door. It was a big lot. The building had six doors, one on the north side, one on the south side, and two each on the east and west sides. She usually came out of the door at the southeast side. He drove up and down the east parking lot looking for her car while trying not to cause any attention, as he knew security guards drove around checking for anything suspicious. Sometimes he would drive slowly past and just look down the aisles but occasionally he would drive down the aisles. Finally he reached the other end of the building and turned into a second parking lot that the employees would use to enter the door at the north end of the building. This parking lot was not so big as there was just one entrance to the building. He saw her car. So she *was* trying to trick him.

Sarah walked the full length of her building and once out in the parking lot she looked around but didn't see the black car.

She was so thankful to have Gloria as her friend. She was always willing to give up her time when she could for Sarah. A desk clerk who used an intercom to announce visitors secured the apartment building. He rang Gloria's number and told her that a Sarah was here to see her. Gloria told him she was expecting her and to send her up. They were both so happy to see each other when Gloria opened her door. They hugged for a long time.

"Come in! Let me have a look at you," said Gloria at first happy and then she put on a sad look. "You don't look like you are taking good care of yourself. You look tired and have lost weight. Now I taught you better than that," she said pretending to scold Sarah.

"I am tired, Gloria. Life is not being good to me right now," Sarah admitted.

"Sit down, I have a shrimp salad in the refrigerator. Let me get it and you can tell me what has been going on."

"This is a wonderful salad," Sarah said as she shared with Gloria what had been happening.

"How strange. It sounds like someone is stalking you. Have you gone to the police?"

"Yes, Tyler's uncle is a detective for the Austin Police Department. We had him over for dinner one night and shared everything. He took the notes that I received but I think it will be hard to find who sent them. They were typed on a word processor and many people have the same type of printer, so unless there was something weird about it, I think it is almost impossible to trace."

"Are there no fingerprints?"

"No! Apparently he was careful. Probably wore those plastic medical gloves. Even the photograph of Sam and me had only mine and Tyler's fingerprints on it."

"So what caused you and Tyler to break up? Did he not believe you?"

"There was so much stress between us. I could see he was fretting too much. He was worried about me and felt he had to be there for me but it was at the cost of losing some business. I felt that if we didn't separate, the cancer would grow and we would not be able to heal." Then with a more hopeful note she said, "We are still in touch and intend getting back together. He calls me every day on my cell phone. I don't always answer though. I'm afraid I will give in to his pleadings for me to return. Maybe after a time of being apart, all this nonsense will stop and we can get back together and back to our lives."

"I'm sorry, honey. It seems like a nightmare."

"It is my worst nightmare Gloria. Enough about me, I want to know what is happening to your movie career."

"Before we leave the subject, I would definitely advise you to keep in touch with Tyler. Answer the phone and talk to him when he calls. He and his uncle are the ones you need to depend on right now," said Gloria with concern. "As for me, I am in the midst of filming and Martin is directing. I told you I was seeing him didn't I?"

"Yes you did and I'm so happy for you, Gloria. I can tell you are in a good place in your life. You deserve it," Sarah said sincerely. They talked on for quite a while then Sarah decided it was time to leave. It was ten o'clock. Gloria wanted to walk her to the front door of the apartment building. Sarah told her not to bother that she would be fine but Gloria insisted. She wanted to make sure her little friend got to her car safely.

"Goodnight Gloria," she said hugging her. Thank you for listening to me, but now please go back inside it's cold out here."

"I will. Drive carefully, Sarah and answer the phone when Tyler calls."

Sarah nodded and walked to her car. As she was driving off she rolled down her window and told Gloria to go inside. They waved. Just before turning the corner she looked back and saw that Gloria was still standing outside. She seemed to be checking something out.

"Go in, Gloria," she said aloud to herself.

It was Saturday morning and Tyler was glad not to have to go to work. It had been almost impossible for him to think because of his concern for Sarah. He had just poured a cup of coffee when the doorbell rang. He put his coffee down and walked to the door. It was pretty early for any of his family to be visiting. He opened the door to find Uncle Dan. He looked a little grim.

"Come on in. Have you come up with something?"

"I need to get a hold of Sarah. I have tried calling her cell phone but she doesn't answer."

"What do you need her for?"

"We will explain at the station when we get a hold of Sarah." Dan Rogers trusted his nephew but in this situation he didn't know what Tyler would do.

Tyler pulled his cell phone from his pocket and dialed. He actually was surprised that she answered.

"Sarah, Tyler here. Uncle Dan has been trying to get a hold of you. You need to get down to the police station. He needs to talk to you. I will be there too."

"Tyler, I just got out of the shower. I didn't get his call. What is it about?"

"I don't know. Just meet us there as soon as you can."

Tyler was already there when Sarah arrived. Dan ushered them both into his office and closed the door. He had his partner with him. He walked around his desk and sat down. He didn't like what he had to say. He stared at them for a few seconds. They both looked scared. Tyler took Sarah's hand as though to reassure her that everything would be okay, but he didn't look very confident.

"Sarah, where were you last night?" Dan asked.

Tyler looked confused, first at Dan then at Sarah. This wasn't the kind of questioning he was expecting.

"After work I went to visit my friend Gloria, then about ten o'clock I went home to my apartment and was by myself the rest of the evening," Sarah replied then looked at Tyler as though needing an explanation.

"Uncle Dan, would you get to the point? This is obviously killing both Sarah and me," Tyler asked impatiently.

"What was the last thing you and Gloria did? I mean the very last thing before you left her and where exactly were you?"

"I don't understand," she said looking around once more at Tyler.

"Please, Sarah you have to answer," Dan said.

"She was a little worried about me going to my car by myself so she insisted on coming down to the parking lot with me. Even though we are very good friends, she insists on mothering me. I was parked just across from the front door of the apartment building and she stood by the door watching me until I started my car up. I rolled down my window and told her to go inside and she said she would."

"So she was still outside when you left?"

"Yes! I remember as I was turning the corner I looked back in my rear mirror and she was still out there but she was not looking after me. She had her head turned the other way. I begged her to get back into her building." She had the terrible feeling something bad had happened. She turned ashen, "Please tell me that Gloria is okay."

"I'm sorry, Sarah. Gloria is dead." There was no way to make it easy for her. She sat staring at Dan with a blank look on her face as though she hadn't heard him or it didn't kick in then she started to slump forward but Tyler caught her. Dan poured her a glass of water and handed it to Tyler. She drank a little of the water then sat staring blankly once again at Dan Rogers.

"How did she die?" Sarah finally asked with a small shaky voice.

"She was stabbed to death." Tyler sat in his chair speechless. *What is going on in Sarah's life? Why are so many ugly things happening to her?* Tyler thought.

"In her apartment?" Sarah inquired.

"No! It was right outside of the door and according to the desk clerk, you were the last person to be with her."

"Uncle Dan, surely you are not suggesting that Sarah would commit such a horrible crime? Gloria was her best friend." Tyler was indignant.

"I'm not suggesting anything, Tyler. We just have to go by the facts," said Dan then turning to Sarah. "The clerk saw you leave in your car and a few minutes later Gloria fell in front of the door. He went out to help her but realized she was already dead," Dan continued.

"How can that be? I didn't see any one there with her when I looked in my mirror," Sarah said. Her head was hurting and her mind couldn't seem to grasp what was being said. None of it made sense.

"The clerk called us. He told us about the other woman but he only knew her as Sarah, so we went up to Gloria's apartment to look for clues. We saw the two used plates and two glasses. On her calendar, which was lying by the phone, she had written 'Sarah–dinner at 6:00 pm with a phone number which I recognized as yours, Tyler. Why did she have your number and not Sarah's?"

"She didn't know Tyler and I were separated until I told her last night," Sarah answered.

"Did you and Gloria have an argument?" Dan's partner finally spoke up.

Before Sarah could answer, Tyler blurted out, "Wait a minute John . . ."

"Tyler" his uncle interrupted "We have to ask the questions. How fast do you think you were going when you left her?"

"The speed limit through the parking lot is ten miles per hour and I was not going faster than that because I was watching to see if she would go inside. I'm sorry that I didn't go back because I was concerned about her being outside. I knew the desk clerk was right there, so I felt she was okay."

"We will talk to the clerk again and see if we can find out any more clues, meanwhile Sarah you know you can't leave the area? I would suggest that you move back home."

"I don't want to cause Tyler . . ." she didn't get to finish.

"If you don't go back home I see no other alternative than to put you in a safe house," Dan interrupted.

"Sarah, we have to worry about you. I can take care of myself. In fact I am worse with you outside on your own. I worry even more," Tyler said.

"It seems to me that this person has been trying to split you two up all along. Perhaps figuring that would be a way of getting you alone Sarah. It looks like you are in terrible danger."

Sarah was numb. There was nothing else she could add to the events of last evening. Her best friend was dead and perhaps it was because of her visit.

"Okay," she agreed.

Both she and Tyler stood up and Sarah's legs gave way from under her. She felt sick to her stomach. Tyler grabbed her once again and steadied her.

Once outside Sarah said, "I don't have to move back right now. I put everyone's life in danger."

"Oh, yes you do. I don't want to let you out of my sight. Sarah. Do you realize how close you might have been to the person who killed Gloria? It could have been you," he said angrily although not really at her. He was angry at the whole situation and he couldn't help her. He wished he could find the person who was trying to hurt her. He turned to her and said more softly, "Give me your keys. You don't look like you are in any condition to drive." She handed him her keys. She was still unsteady so he put his arm around her and helped her into the car.

Once in the car Sarah said, "I probably led the killer to Gloria's apartment."

"Don't do this Sarah. None of this was your fault. Did you see the black car behind you?" he asked.

She had to think for a moment. She knew she had been looking for it when she came out of her work but it hadn't been anywhere around. Then she remembered looking for it on the freeway but once again, she didn't see it.

"No, there was a red truck directly behind me that blocked my view. I couldn't see what was behind it."

They sat quietly driving along when suddenly Sarah put her hands up to her face, covering her eyes and started to sob.

"Do you want me to pull over?"

She shook her head, "No!"

He kept driving and after about ten minutes Sarah stopped crying. Her stomach was turning and she began to salivate. She knew she was going to throw up. He looked at her and noticed she had gotten terribly pale. He pulled the car over in a quiet road next to a field. She opened the door and fell to her knees on the ground and started throwing up. Tyler grabbed her tissues and her bottle of water and ran to the other side of the car to assist her. He put his arms around her ribs and helped hold her up while she vomited.

He felt helpless. Who was this monster who was trying to destroy her life? If only he knew who he was he would go after him personally and get rid of him in some way.

A police car pulled over and two policemen got out to investigate. Officer Jerry Maxwell recognized Tyler. "Hey Tyler. Is everything okay?" he asked.

"Hi Jerry. She'll be okay. She got some bad news that has upset her." He helped her up and washed her face and mouth with a water soaked tissue.

"Okay, well we'll leave you alone. Take care of her." They drove away and Tyler helped Sarah back into the car.

Sarah moved back home. They tried to live as normally as possible but it was hard. They felt like locking themselves behind their door but knew they couldn't allow themselves to be terrorized by this monster. Sam had suggested to Tyler that Sarah take off the rest of the year and when the New Year came they would re-evaluate her situation to see if she needed more time. She had not been functioning well at work. Sam told him that John was willing to give her as much time as it took to get back to normal. He told Tyler that Sarah was a very important part of their team but he and John were willing to do anything to help her.

Attending Gloria's funeral was extremely difficult for Sarah. Everyone from the agency was there. She couldn't help feeling guilty for her death and wondered how her friends felt. She had a hard time lifting her head up. When they put the coffin into the ground she felt faint. If it hadn't been for Tyler holding her up she knew she would hit the ground. After the ceremony was over most people from the agency came over to her to give her a hug and say a few words. Gloria's boyfriend, Martin, seemed to be in shock. He just stood the whole time looking at the coffin as though he didn't believe that his Gloria was in there. Some of the people from the agency went over and introduced themselves and offered condolences. Sarah was having a difficult time going over to offer her condolences but she knew it was the kind thing to do.

"Martin, I am Sarah. I was with Gloria the night this awful thing happened," she said, her voice shaking.

"Hello Sarah! Gloria spoke of you with much respect," he said.

"I am terribly sorry," was all she could say. What else! It was devastating to everyone and nobody knew what to do. There was nothing to do. Gloria was gone and they couldn't bring her back. It was final.

CHAPTER 24

It was almost Christmas and neither of them had the right spirit. Tyler felt so bad because Sarah seemed to be becoming more and more depressed. He took her shopping but her heart just wasn't in it. He made a few choices on gifts for his mom and dad and Kevin and his niece and nephew. He already had Sarah's gift hidden away in the house. Now he just had to get a gift for his brother and his wife and sister and her husband. He tried to make her happy but nothing worked. She hadn't even bought anything for her parents. Tyler had set up some counseling meetings with Pastor Jones but he wasn't sure that was getting to her either. Of course they had only had two meetings. The pastor had talked about the guilt she was feeling and tried to help her let go. As strong as Sarah was, she couldn't carry the weight of the guilt and the loss. Tyler was extremely worried about her. At least she was not going to work right now so he felt pretty secure about her safety. She had promised she would not go out alone, but her spirit was getting lower and lower. He was afraid if she didn't snap out of this depression, he might not be able to reach her.

Meanwhile, Dan Rogers and his partner went to the Canto Agency to talk with Mike Carter. They sat across from Mike's desk.

"Do you know of any problems Gloria was having with anyone?" Dan asked.

"No! Definitely not anyone at the agency. Everyone liked her. She was very professional which made everyone, like the photographer for example, love working with her. She made their jobs easier."

"How about the other models? Any jealousy?"

"No! Gloria gave advice to the girls, but only when they asked. She never imposed her point of view on anyone."

"How about her relationship with Sarah Kincaid?"

"Detective, we all know that Sarah got picked up for questioning. She is the last person you should suspect. She and Gloria were like sisters. Sarah depended on Gloria for a lot of advice inside and outside of the profession."

"Sarah has been having trouble for quite a while with someone stalking her and sending notes that has caused stress and her eventual moving out of her home. Thankfully she and Tyler are back together but they are still under a lot of stress. With the murder of Gloria the night that Sarah was with her makes us suspicious that maybe it has something to do with the stalking incidents. We are just trying to put two and two together. Also the fact that both of them were models and worked here . . ."

"I wish I could be of more help, Detective Rogers. If I can be of any help at all, all of us here at Canto will surely make ourselves available, but at the moment I am clueless. I will certainly call you if something comes up."

Standing up Dan put out his hand to Mike. Mike stood up and shook his hand.

Tyler sat in his office trying to decide how he could bring Sarah back from this horrible place she had gone to. *What can I do? I have never known anyone to be in the mental condition Sarah is in.* Kevin walked in. He looked at Tyler and knew he was worrying about Sarah. Kevin was worried too.

"Things still not looking up for Sarah?" he inquired.

"No, Kev, she seems to be getting worse every day. I'm trying to think of how to bring her back to her old self."

"It would seem that it shouldn't take too much. Sarah had so little in her life that it would seem that almost anything would excite her."

"She does get excited over little things normally, but I don't know what would excite her now," Tyler confessed feeling helpless.

"Well you know the Trail of Lights begins this Sunday. Sarah has never seen anything like that, I can assure you."

"Hey Kev, I forgot all about that. That sounds like a great idea. Thanks."

Tyler waited until he got home, instead of calling to tell her. He was quite excited about the idea and hoped it would bring a sparkle back to her usually bright eyes.

"Sarah, I'm going to take you to the Trail of Lights at Zilker Park this Sunday. It will be the opening event when the tree lights get turned on. I think you will really enjoy it."

"Okay sweetheart that will be nice," Sarah said trying to sound interested. She knew how hard this was on him and decided she would try and have a good time on Sunday.

As they entered the park there was a huge lighted sign overhead welcoming everyone. It sparked something in her. She had never seen such a beautiful sight before. "Wow!"

Tyler was glad to get the littlest response from her. There were a lot of people in the park. Lots of young families with excited children running about. It was a very happy time for them. Sarah found herself thinking that she wished *she* were happy. Tyler thought being that she was an engineer, reading some statistics from the brochure about the tree might be interesting to her.

"This is one of the world's largest man-made trees. It's 155 feet tall and 180 feet in diameter. It has over 3,500 bulbs." They got to the tree about ten minutes before the lights came on. She was impressed with the facts that Tyler shared with her but to see the tree was even more impressive.

I wish I could feel more excited about this, she thought. She just felt numb.

When it came time to light the tree, people started counting down. "Five . . . four . . . three . . . two . . . one . . . lights," the people yelled and finally it seemed like the whole park was in living color. It took her breath away. She felt like a child in some magical place. She had never seen such a sight. Her father had tried to take her to various events when she was a child but her mother made a fuss over such frivolity that her father gave in, so she never experienced anything like this. She was in awe. Tyler turned to see what her reaction was and found her staring up like a child. Her mouth was open and her eyes were shining. He was thrilled to see her looking excited for a change with that little girl expression. He knew she had never experienced anything like it.

I am sure Sarah probably hasn't had any exciting experiences as a child, he thought. He kept silent and just watched her as tears rolled down her cheeks. She didn't even try and wipe them away. She hadn't cried since the day in the car when they got the news of Gloria. It was as if something was breaking through. He just left her alone not wanting to disturb her but wanting to give her this time to herself. She turned to him and smiled, a very soft smile.

"Oh Tyler, this is the most beautiful scene I have ever witnessed," she said and turned back to the lights. He put his arm around her shoulders and held her close. He decided not to talk but to let her experience whatever emotion she was having. He was just happy to see emotion.

"I'm afraid to look away unless they go out." The parade brought even broader smiles to her face and more tears. She would clap as different groups or bands would pass by. When the parade was finished they walked the one-mile trail with thirty-eight or so lighted scenes. She was cold but she would never have left for anything. He felt her shiver and took off his jacket and put it over her shoulders. The lights, the parade, the merriment all seemed to awaken something in Sarah. It was the Christmas season, the time for giving. For Sarah it was a time for giving thanks. She still had people that loved her. Whoever this ugly person was he couldn't take that from her. *Gloria would not have wanted me to go on mourning forever. She would have been the first person to tell me to move forward,* Sarah thought.

Tyler was surprised when after they got home she said, "Do you think we could have Christmas dinner here?"

"Of course darling. I think that's an excellent idea," he answered his heart full of joy that she was showing signs of life.

"Great! We should go shopping tomorrow for a tree and decorations."

"You mean you want to do all the work of decorating. Are you sure you are up to it?"

"Yes, dear I am and you will help me," she smiled at him.

Decorating the house and planning for Christmas dinner actually was therapy for her. She still had moments of depression but she knew she was on her way to healing. The tree was beautifully decorated with different colored lights. She didn't want to have a color theme. She wanted the tree to have all the Christmas colors and more. The mantelpiece had red candles and Christmas topiaries with a centerpiece of fir, holly and mistletoe, and on the hearth on each side of the fireplace were poinsettias. The banister going upstairs had a pine runner all the way up with red bows and holly and mistletoe. They had candles all over the house, including the bathroom. It was Tyler's job to buy the appetizers and beverages on Christmas Eve while Sarah decorated the dining table. It had a red MacAulay tartan runner down the center on top of the red tablecloth and she made sure the centerpiece was low, so everyone could see each other. She was glad that Tyler had good taste in dinnerware and glassware. She put nameplates by each place so that everyone knew where they were to sit. She was feeling rather excited even though she still felt sad about Gloria; but once again she reminded herself that Gloria would not want her mourning all the time. She would want Sarah to enjoy this first Christmas with Tyler and his family

John Kincaid was tired this night. He had had a busier than usual day at work. *After dinner I'm going to take a book upstairs and go right to bed,* he thought. As he was putting his briefcase on the credenza in the hall, he noticed an envelope with Sarah's return name and address. It was unopened. He picked it up and walked into the living room. "This is from Sarah. Why didn't you open it?" he said rather short because he was tired and fed up with Olivia's up and down attitude toward their daughter. She didn't answer him so he opened the envelope and said "We have been invited to their home for Christmas dinner."

"I don't celebrate Christmas," she replied in a bored tone.

"Well I do. I will be going and I think that you should go too. Sarah has been a wonderful daughter to us and we have not been exactly wonderful to her," he said getting short with her. "I'm so glad she has snapped out of the depression she was in," he said changing his tone and thinking what a relief it was to him. "Tyler took her to Zilker Park to see the Trail of Lights tree lighting and parade. He said she was so in awe of the sight that it brought her emotions back."

"Sarah was always childlike about such frivolity."

"She just knows how to enjoy life, Olivia," he said. "You should just be happy that something brought her back, regardless of whether you think it silly or not."

"She wouldn't have had to go through all that grief if she would have stayed here in Marshallville," she said in a rather I-told-you-so voice.

"She's a very successful and happy young woman and you still would rather have her back here going to that weird church and looking like a frumpy old biddy." She cast a shocked look at him that made him wish he had not said that but he had had it. He grabbed his book and went upstairs, foregoing dinner.

Sarah was so excited on Christmas day. She remembered the other time when she felt excited about having company for dinner. Tyler turned to say something to her and found her looking at him. "What?" then he remembered. He walked over to her and put his arms around her. "Don't worry baby, I would never think of spoiling this day. I love you very, very much and what's her name is totally out of the picture."

"I'm sorry Tyler. I don't know why the picture of our cookout flashed in my head."

The doorbell rang and most of Tyler's family came around the same time. Christmas music was playing in the background and all of a sudden the house was full of voices and laughter. This was going to be the first real Christmas Sarah had experienced. Her mother didn't believe in holidays, so her father used to take her over to his brother's home where they would have dinner with his family. Even though Uncle Andrew and his family loved having them, she always felt sort of like an outsider. She was glad that her dad had called to say that he would come but she was afraid that somehow her mother would find a way to keep him from doing so. The doorbell rang and her heart leapt to her throat. When she opened it she was thrilled to see her dad. This time he was having Christmas dinner at his daughter's home.

"Daddy, I'm so glad you came. Come in." John gave her a huge hug. There were no excuses given as to why Olivia was not there and nobody asked. He shook hands with the men and kissed the women on the cheek wishing them all a Merry Christmas. The MacAulays knew it would embarrass John to inquire about Olivia. After all this was her daughter's first Christmas dinner as a married woman and in her own home.

She should be here, thought Alice MacAulay. *After all Sarah has been through, her mother should definitely be here.* John put presents under the tree with the help of Alice MacAulay. She wanted to get him alone to tell him how impressed she was with Sarah.

"Sarah looks wonderful John. It is so good to see her eyes shine again. We were all so worried. Tyler was afraid he was losing her."

"We all did, Alice. It was just so out of sorts for Sarah. She is a strong girl but losing her friend the way she did was too much for her."

"Well I'll get on my brother to keep priority on this case," she promised him.

For dinner they cooked a pork loin roast with apples and sautéed red cabbage, courtesy of Martha Stewart. Tyler felt proud of Sarah for all the work she had put into making this a wonderful day in spite of the fact that he knew her heart was still aching. She looked beautiful in her teal colored dress. She wore the diamond pendant and earrings that he had bought her for her birthday. He couldn't believe this was the same little girl who was on her knees on the street throwing up just about three weeks ago.

Tyler wanted to toast her. He raised his glass, "Sarah I am very impressed. You did a wonderful job decorating the house and the meal was scrumptious."

Alice MacAulay couldn't help but admire her also and let her know.

"I am very touched that you brought a little of the MacAulay tartan to the table with your runner," Ian MacAulay said. "Tyler's grandpa would be proud."

"Tyler did a lot of the work also," Sarah said not wanting to take all of the credit.

"But all the creativity came from you, " Tyler said making sure everyone knew how hard she had worked.

Her dad sat quiet. He had so many emotions going on. He was certainly very proud of her but he was sad that he hadn't been a better father to her. He raised his glass "I want to toast my daughter also. She is a remarkable woman. She has overcome many obstacles in her young life," *including the childhood she had had,* he thought, "and I am very proud of her."

Tyler and Sarah knew all the obstacles he was talking about. Sarah felt so close to her dad at that moment. She was glad that he made his own decision to come in spite of her mom.

Everyone helped clean up the dishes so it didn't take too long. After cleanup they went into the living room and exchanged gifts. Tyler handed John a present, which surprised and thrilled Sarah. She had not done any shopping. When John opened it there was a lovely pair of leather riding boots. John was so touched he went over and gave Tyler a hug. It brought tears to Sarah's eyes to see the two men that she loved sharing such an emotional moment. Tyler gave her riding boots and a fleece lined suede jacket. Sarah hadn't bought very much for Tyler due to the mental condition she was in prior to Christmas and she felt embarrassed and apologized to him.

"Darlin, everything you did to make this such a perfect day is all I need. And, by the way, I have to say you look stunning," he said lifting his glass and smiling at her. John Kincaid was more than happy to raise his glass. He was thrilled with the way things turned out for her. She had a doting husband and was welcomed into his family. Everyone was thrilled with their gifts and passed them around for everyone else to see. After they were through looking at each other's gifts, Tyler got up and walked out of the room. When he came back he walked over to Sarah.

"This is my real gift to you," he said getting down on his knees and handing her a box with a beautiful platinum engagement ring with a one-carat diamond. Since they got married quickly, they didn't have the time to pick out a diamond ring, so they settled on plain platinum bands for each of them. He was going through the gesture of proposing since he didn't do that either. They were both so anxious to be together that a lot of the formalities went by the wayside but Tyler wanted to make up for some of them.

"Tyler, it is the most beautiful engagement ring . . ." she stopped as she became emotional. Her dad handed her some Kleenex. He even took one for himself. Everyone gasped at the ring. He took it from the box and placed it on her finger with the wedding band. Ian MacAulay was taking movies with his new digital camcorder.

"Thank you Tyler," she said standing up to kiss him and helping him to his feet. "I will marry you over and over again." Everyone clapped.

"It is beautiful, Tyler. Did you pick it out by yourself?" his mom asked.

"Yes, when I saw it I thought, that ring has Sarah's name on it." Everyone went over to Sarah to admire the ring.

"The next thing we have to do is pick a time and place for our honeymoon," he said. It was a touching moment and everyone was either smiling or crying.

"We could never have asked for a more wonderful daughter-in-law than Sarah," Alice said looking at John Kincaid. "We all love her very much." She walked over to Sarah, hugged her and said, "I am glad you said yes when Tyler asked you to marry him. Once more, welcome to the family. You too John, welcome."

After Tyler's family left, John, who was staying with them decided it was time for him to go to bed.

"I really can't thank you enough baby for giving us all such a wonderful day. I was bursting with pride at the way the decorations, the meal, *everything* turned out."

She kissed him. "Thank you for taking me to Zilker Park. And thank you again for this beautiful ring."

When John got home he told Olivia that Tyler had given Sarah a diamond engagement ring.

"It was a very touching moment. I wish you had been there and I'm sure Sarah wished you had too."

"Something in me wished I had too but I don't think I would have been comfortable. It sounded like you had a good time. I am glad they are happy and she has gotten over her depression." Sometimes Olivia sounded almost reasonable and John would hope things would get better but then she would go back to her old self.

"Tyler gave me a great pair of riding boots. I left them at their house, as that is where I'll be using them. He also bought you a gift. Here," he said handing her a gift-wrapped box.

"You know I don't celebrate Christmas. What am I going to do with a gift? Now I suppose I will have to write a thank you note," she complained.

"You won't know what you are going to do with it until you open it and a thank you note would be nice, but Tyler wouldn't hold it against you if you didn't send one."

She tore off the wrapping paper with a look of annoyance. *Why did he do this, it puts me in an awkward spot,* she was thinking. She couldn't imagine what he could have bought her. The box said Pfaltzgraff Pistoulet Pedestal Cake Plate. She opened the box. The colors and design took her breath away for a moment and her annoyed looked actually turned into one of delight. It was exactly her style, very country-folksy.

"Well are you going to show it to me?" John's curiosity was getting the better of him. He had noticed her countenance had changed. He couldn't imagine what anyone would get Olivia. You certainly couldn't buy her clothes, perfume or makeup. Maybe a little trinket for the house, he thought. When she lifted it out he was once again touched by Tyler's sensitivity.

"He knows you love to bake and what a perfect match for your kitchen. He remembered that your walls are yellow and your cabinets are indigo blue."

"Well Sarah probably told him."

"Sarah didn't even know he had bought us presents. I bet she doesn't even know what you got. She wasn't in the right frame of mind to shop so he did it for her. That's what kind of son-in-law we have."

"I think I will send that thank you note after all. I truly love this cake stand." John thought maybe this could be the breakthrough that she needed. Tyler couldn't have picked a better gift for her.

Each day Tyler noticed that Sarah was coming more and more out of the depression. The lighting of the tree at the park, plus having her dad at her home for Christmas and the engagement ring had all helped to bring light back to her beautiful eyes. Nothing seemed to light them up more though than the note that came to Tyler four days after Christmas. He opened it to make sure it wouldn't hurt her feelings then he called her in to the living room. When she came in she noticed he was holding an envelope. "What is it?"

"It's a note from your mom."

"For me?" She was surprised since her mom never sent her notes.

"No it's for me."

" I hope she is nice to you," making a face indicating she was afraid of what her mother had written to Tyler.

He took the note out, opened it and read: "Tyler, thank you for sending me a gift for Christmas by way of my husband. I am not used to accepting gifts or sending notes,"

Sarah held her breath at the last sentence. *What was going to come next*, she thought.

Tyler continued, "but I have to say that it was very sensitive of you. I know I am not an easy person to buy for but you knew exactly what to buy. The fact that you took into account that my kitchen is very dear to me and the colors are yellow and blue and the style country, the cake plate was perfect. It is very lovely and I do thank you for taking time to find something so perfect for me. Olivia Kincaid." When he looked at Sarah she was staring at him with her mouth and eyes wide open. "I can't believe my mother wrote that. Why didn't you let me know you had bought my parents gifts? I feel bad that I didn't do anything."

CHAPTER 25

On New Year's Eve they decided to have a quiet time and just have Kevin and his girlfriend Kelly over. They watched a few funny movies then Kevin and Tyler went into the game room and played some pool. "I wish I could have been here when you gave Sarah the engagement ring. I hope someone took a video of you doing that. I want to see all the expressions."

"My dad got a digital camcorder for Christmas so he was taking movies of everything and he got me giving Sarah the ring. We will show it to you tonight."

"I'm glad everything is going well for you both," Kevin said sincerely.

"Well, I wish I could keep her home all the time, but that would not be fair. She loves her work, but the murdering scumbag is still out there and we still have no clues."

"Let's hope this New Year will bring an end to all of it."

"I think that will be my New Year's resolution," Tyler said.

"What do you mean?" Kevin asked.

"My New Year's resolution will be to resolve," he said jokingly. They were still laughing when the women came in.

"What is going on in here? We want to be part of the fun too," complained Sarah teasingly.

"Oh, it wasn't even funny. Just a stupid remark at trying to make light of a heavy thing."

"What?" asked Sarah confused.

"Nothing. Not worth going there."

"Okay! Then why don't we go into the family room? The ball will drop in Times Square in approximately ten minutes," Sarah suggested.

After hugging and kissing and wishing each other Happy New Year, Tyler brought out the video and showed it to Kevin and Kelly. Kevin could see his buddy doing that; getting down on his knees as though proposing while presenting Sarah with the ring in front of everyone. He wasn't shy about anything. Kevin wasn't sure that he could have got down on his knees in front of everyone. "You mean Conor didn't make a joke? Look at him, he actually looks like he is about to cry," Kevin said laughing. Tyler had taken the camera from his dad and made sure he and Sarah's dads were in the video too.

"Oh look, how touching. My dad has tears in his eyes," Sarah remarked. Kevin had never seen his Uncle John looking so emotional. He was quite touched by it but he also saw how happy he was.

"Could I get a copy to take to my parents? I would especially like my dad to see his brother looking so happy and being so comfortable with his new family." After he said it he wanted to bite his tongue. His dad always felt bad for his brother, especially at Christmas when he would bring his daughter over to their house because his wife didn't celebrate the holiday. But he hadn't meant to blurt it out in front of Sarah. Tyler knew Kevin felt bad, so he quickly changed the subject.

"Okay enough of the emotional stuff let's get some humor going."

They sat around the fire talking and sharing funny stories. "Who is your favorite TV comic?" asked Kevin of everyone. They thought hard about it. "That is a difficult question," answered Tyler. "There are so many great comics, but one of my favorites is Bob Newhart. I love watching all his old shows. He used to have a show where he was the only one in it. He would do all the skits himself. It was a riot but later he had a show where he played a psychiatrist. Have any of you seen that show?"

"I've seen it a number of times. It was a funny show," Kevin replied.

"Did you see the one where he and his buddies had a little too much to drink and they are trying to order Chinese food to be delivered? He is on the phone placing the order," Tyler was laughing just remembering the scene, "but when it came to ordering Goo Moo Pai Gan. He tries to say it about a half a dozen times and it keeps coming out wrong. They are all laughing so hard tears are rolling down their faces. You can't help but sit there and laugh with them. You feel like you are right there being a part of their hilarity."

"What in the world is Moo Goo Pan Gan?" Kevin asked.

Tyler cracked up laughing. "You can't say it either. I said, "Goo Goo . . . No wait a minute . . . Goo Moo Gan Pai . . . Jeez, how do you say the stupid thing?" By this time they were all laughing hard, especially Kevin and Tyler. Kelly and Sarah decided they were not going to help them out because they were enjoying themselves so much watching these two guys falling off their chairs and laughing 'til their sides ached.

After they composed themselves Kelly said, "one of my favorite funny scenes on television was on the Mary Tyler Moore show when they were attending the funeral service for Chuckles the clown. Whenever the minister would mention the name Chuckles, Mary would try and hold back a giggle. After a while it got to the point where she was unable to hold back and pretty soon the minister says, 'It's okay to laugh, young lady, that is what Chuckles would want so go ahead'. Then instead of laughing she bursts out crying. You have to see it to get the humor."

"That was a funny scene. I saw that episode too," Tyler said. "Has anyone here ever been in a serious situation where you wanted to giggle but felt it wouldn't be appropriate?" They thought about it.

"Well, one time in church, I think I was about thirteen," Sarah said trying to remember, "I was around that age anyway you know when girls are very giggly. I was sitting there with my bored face on, my eyes rolling and yawning. I didn't know the man next to me had fallen asleep. He must have had a dream or something. Anyway there I am sitting bored stiff and he jumps in his seat and kicks the bottom of the seat in front of him. It scared the living daylights out of me and I jumped and the man in front whose seat got kicked jumped. After a few moments everyone was acting as though nothing had happened but I was giggling and couldn't stop. I had to run out of the church."

They were all laughing. Everyone could relate to the story in some way. "You're mother must have been furious with you," Tyler said still laughing.

"She was. She told my dad and he started laughing too which made mother even more furious."

They spent the next couple of hours telling stories and having a good time. Finally around three o'clock they decided to retire. "I hope I can get to sleep," said Tyler.

"Why wouldn't you? It's two-thirty and I know you were up early this morning," Kevin replied.

"I can't stop thinking about Moo Goo Gai Pan . . . hey that's it! Moo Goo Gai Pan, Moo Goo Gai Pan" he kept saying it and then Kevin joined in and pretty soon it was like a chant. Finally Sarah grabbed Tyler by the elbow and led him to the bedroom.

They slept until ten o'clock the next morning. Sarah had gotten up earlier and made a big pot of coffee.

"I had the best time ever last night. I haven't laughed so much in so long," Kevin said. "One thing I definitely won't forget—" he continued looking very melancholy.

"What's that?" Tyler inquired.

Kevin looked up at Tyler with a very sad looking face and said, "Moo Goo Gai Pan." The laughter started up again.

"You two better stop. My mother said that when you laugh too much you will end up crying," Sarah said.

"Oh, your mother is full of all kinds of weird sayings," answered Tyler. Then turning to Kevin, "Can you and Kelly stay around a while? We thought we would go horseback riding in the afternoon."

"No, we have to get going. Kelly is getting ready right now. We promised to stop by and wish her folks a Happy New Year and then we are driving to Marshallville to see my folks, but thanks anyway. I wouldn't have been anywhere else but here last night. It truly was great." Tyler patted his back and asked Sarah for another round of coffee since she was up on her feet.

Pouring them both some fresh coffee she turned to Kevin "It was great for us having you both here. I've really been realizing even more these past few weeks, how important family and friends are. When you get home, give my New Year's greetings to your family for me."

"Why don't you take the video to them. If they want a copy we can make one when you bring it back to us," Tyler suggested.

"Talking about family I better call mine."

Sarah hung up the phone and sighed. "Is everything okay?" Tyler asked.

"Yes, you know my mom she worries about everything. Now she worries about me flying around the world, as she puts it. She is afraid of terrorists. She said she has Reverend Barker pray for me every time I get on a plane."

"Oh, here's Kelly," Kevin said. "Are you ready to go?"

"Yes." Kelly answered. They hugged and said their goodbyes.

Later in the afternoon Tyler and Sarah went riding. She felt good in her new boots and jacket. Tyler had a jacket similar to hers and he wore a cowboy hat. She couldn't help thinking how rugged he looked sitting up on his horse looking so tall and strong. He was so manly looking, much different from the guy falling off his chair laughing the night before. She had never seen him and Kevin like that before. They both had such a similar sense of humor. Kelly had confided in her that she was sure she was in love with Kevin. Sarah secretly hoped they would get married. She would like all four of them to always be as close as they were last night. She wished this year would bring everything in her life back to normal.

"I'm going back to work in a week coming Monday," she announced.

"What made you decide that?" he asked with concern.

"That was the agreement. John said we would re-evaluate at the beginning of the year. There have been no incidents since Gloria's death at the beginning of December so I thought it would be okay to go back. John won't be back in the office until Monday, so I will call him then."

"It has only been a month since Gloria's death. Besides you haven't been to work since then so he hasn't been able to follow you."

"He knows where I live."

"That's different. Your schedule varies while you're here. You don't walk out of the door around the same time every night into a public parking lot. Besides when you're home, I usually am too. He wouldn't take that kind of chance."

"Tyler, I have to go back some day. I'm feeling a need to get back to normal."

"I'm feeling a need to have you with me for a long time."

"You haven't gone outside by yourself for a while now. I feel safe with you locked up here. I'm nervous about you going back out by yourself," he confessed.

They fell into silence then Tyler spoke up, "Okay, I will talk to Uncle Dan and see what he says. He knows these people better than we do."

"Thanks! Let's not think about it right now. I am enjoying this ride."

CHAPTER 26

Dan Rogers decided, at least for a while, that he would post a couple of his men in an unmarked car in the parking lot between five thirty and six o'clock each night. They would follow Sarah home. Tyler felt good about that. If he was not going to make it home before six thirty, he was sure to call home and check on Sarah. She had been back to work for exactly a week now without anything unusual happening.

The driver of the black car had been very cautious making sure he didn't follow her too close. It was a good thing he did because he noticed that another car with two men in it had been following her also. They would come into the parking lot around five fifteen each night and wait a couple of minutes after she left then they would follow her. This was causing a problem for him. He would watch for another week and if they continued to hang around, he would have to think of another strategy. It was time. He *had* to get her alone.

Sarah left her office and stopped by the secretary's desk. "Barbara I'm leaving a little early since I am going to stop by Arboretum Mall to pick up Elizabeth's baby gift from the staff."

"I didn't realize you were given the job of doing the shopping."

"I volunteered since you guys are putting the whole thing together. Just getting a conference room and the people together at the time you need them is a feat in itself."

Nodding her head Barbara said "Tell me about it."

When she pulled into the mall she decided to check in with Tyler.

"Hi sweetheart, how are you?" she asked.

"I'm fine! What're you up to?"

"I am at the mall. I have to pick up a baby gift for Elizabeth from the staff."

"Sarah, it is only five o'clock. Did you let Uncle Dan know you were leaving early?"

"Oh, Tyler I'm sorry. I forgot. Would you be a dear and let him know so he doesn't send his men out?"

"That's not the point, Sarah. You have pulled yourself out from under their protection. Go straight home."

"I'm already here and it will just be a run in and out since I called the store and had them gift wrap it."

"I'll call Uncle Dan immediately but I want you to know I'm angry at you. He's doing all he can to provide safety for you and you recklessly left your work early before his men got there and then you don't even let him know." His voice was very angry.

"Tyler, I am sorry. I won't do it again. I just didn't think."

"Well get your gift and get your butt home. Don't talk to strangers."

"I will and I won't." She understood why Tyler was so angry. He had a right to be. He was working with his uncle trying to protect her all he could and she was careless. Well she would do exactly like he said; get the gift and get home.

With the gift under her arm, Sarah hurried to her car, opened the trunk and put the gift in. It was too big to put in the back seat. Pushing the unlock button on her key ring she opened the door and threw her purse inside. Just as she was getting ready to get in herself she heard, "Hello Sarah!"

Tyler had called his uncle who said he would call his men Ryan and Jerry and tell them to get over to the mall instead of her work. Tyler had been at work when she called him. He asked Dan if he should also stop in at the mall.

"No, you should head on home right now if you can. As soon as she arrives home, call me and I will let my men know that everything is okay."

Tyler had gone home at lunchtime and put a couple of steaks in a marinade for dinner that night. He had intended on throwing a salad together to go with them but by the time he got home he couldn't think of anything but Sarah. He had tried calling her on her cell phone but she didn't answer. He figured perhaps she had turned it off while in the store, not wanting to bother the other shoppers. That would be just like Sarah. *Jerry and Ryan should be at the mall by now,* he thought. "If all she had to do was run in and pick up the gift, she should be out of the mall by now," he said talking to himself. "She said she was already there when she called me and that was half an hour ago. Why isn't her cell phone on?" He was starting to panic.

Jerry and Ryan were able to park behind her car in the next row. They had called Dan to let him know that her car was still there. Dan in turn called Tyler. He felt relieved that her car was still there and that Jerry and

Ryan were waiting for her. He was upset though that she was taking so long. *She promised me she would run in and out. It's already five-thirty and she hasn't left the mall. She has been there now for thirty minutes. I will really have to have a good talk with her when she gets home. I just pray that she gets home.* His thoughts were running wild by now.

"Women! When they go shopping, it doesn't matter that their life could be in danger you still can't pull them away," Ryan said.

"I don't know, Ryan. I have a funny feeling about this. We both know that she is a very smart, responsible girl. She wouldn't worry Tyler any more by hanging around. I think I'll go and check out her car." Jerry got out and walked over to Sarah's car. Ryan watched him bend over and pick something up. He held up a set of keys. Ryan jumped out of the car and ran over towards him. Jerry tried the door and it was unlocked. He opened it and his heart sank. Inside was Sarah's purse. He pulled it out and showed it to Ryan.

"She ain't shopping." They walked to the back of the car and opened the trunk. Inside they saw a package gift wrapped with baby paper. Jerry got on the phone and called Dan. While he was explaining to Dan about the keys, purse and gift Ryan walked over to him with a white piece of cloth and held it to Jerry's nose.

"Ether" Ryan said.

"Oh, man!" Jerry said in a worried tone.

"What is it Jerry?" Dan was almost barking at him.

"Not good, Dan. Not good at all. Ryan found a piece of cloth near the car soaked in ether."

"I'm on my way. I'll be there in about ten minutes."

Dan was in his car on the way to the mall. He knew he had to call Tyler but this was another of those times when he hated what he had to tell him. He felt sick to his stomach. Tyler picked up the phone.

"Tyler, I'm afraid it's bad news, son."

Tyler's heart sank. He put down his drink. "What is it?"

"I think you should come to the mall."

"Is Sarah dead?" he said in a very faint voice.

"We haven't found her. Just come to the mall."

Tyler hardly remembered the trip to the mall. He was terrified. Feeling very sure that something terrible had happened to Sarah, tears came to his eyes. He couldn't stand the thought of her being hurt or terrified or violated. He had tried to protect her but now he was afraid the monster had his prey. Well he wouldn't get away with it, Tyler vowed to himself. "I will hunt him down like the animal he is and make sure he never hurts another person." He had to force himself to drive the speed limit.

Dan Rogers looked inside the car, then the trunk. They saw the gift. She had done her shopping but just in case she had gone back inside the mall, he had Ryan go and check it out. Although they were sure that didn't happen since her purse was left in the car. After an extensive search and paging they agreed that she wasn't there.

Dan knew how often abductions ended in death. This was the part of his job that he hated. Foul play was bad in any situation but now it was someone he knew and someone very dear to his beloved nephew. All of the family members would be horrified by this news. He just hoped he would find Sarah before anything happened to her. He felt the weight upon his shoulders to find her soon. Tyler arrived and looked over the evidence. He looked desperately at Uncle Dan.

"I'm sorry, Tyler." They talked for a little while. Mostly it was Dan asking questions about he and Sarah's phone conversation, to see if there were any clues. There were none. Dan put his arm around Tyler's shoulders and said "Go home, Tyler; there is nothing you can do. Believe me son, I will put high priority on this one." Tyler picked up the gift and took the keys and purse from Jerry.

Go home. There is nothing you can do. Those words haunted his thoughts. He had never felt so helpless.

He was in a daze when he reached his parent's house. His father knew immediately when he opened the door and saw Tyler standing there looking so pale and frantic, that something terrible had happened.

"Come in son," he said reaching out his hand to him. "Momma, Tyler is here," he called out.

Alice MacAulay came quickly to the entryway with a smile on her face but it quickly disappeared when she saw the wild look in Tyler's eyes. "Darlin', what is wrong?"

He was in a stupor. They led him to the living room couch and set him down. He put his elbow on the arm of the couch and pressed his mouth to his fist. His parents tried to be calm.

"Would you like something to drink, son?" his dad asked. He didn't reply but started sobbing. They had never seen their grown up son cry. They knew it was something bad. They were afraid of the answer should they ask but they knew they had to. He was their son and they had to be strong for him whatever the problem was.

"What is it son?" his dad asked. It took a while for Tyler to regain his composure. Putting his hands between his knees he said, "Sarah is gone." They both thought that she had moved out again, like she did when she was trying to protect Tyler and his job.

"Oh, Tyler, that girl is so crazy about you, she won't stay away for long. Did you have a tiff?" his mother asked with a sigh of relief.

"No mom, Sarah didn't leave me, someone took her." Alice and Ian stared at each other in disbelieve.

"What do you mean Tyler?" his dad asked.

"It looks like she's been abducted. Her keys were found in a parking lot beside her car, her purse was inside and her purchases were in the trunk. She has not been heard from for well over an hour."

"Honey, maybe something else is going on," his mother said trying to convince not only her son that this couldn't be happening but herself also. She was of course aware of the shadow that had been hanging over Sarah for quite a while now, but she had hoped it would never come to this.

"No, something bad has happened to Sarah and I have no idea where to start looking for her. An ether soaked rag was found a little from her car. I promised her I would protect her."

"Son, you can't blame yourself. I know we want to be heroes for our women but you couldn't be with her all the time. I know Dan will do all he possibly can to find her."

"Dad we have no clues. Dan thinks it is someone who knows her. I guess we will have to focus on all her friends and family."

"You don't think that any of her friends or family members would try and hurt her?" his mother asked with such disbelief.

"No, mom. But someone could be giving information about her to someone else, innocently. It's something uncle Dan and I have talked about."

"Honey, you're welcome to stay here tonight if it will make it easier for you," his mother offered.

"Thanks Mom, but I want to be at home in case Sarah or Uncle Dan try to call. I also want to be alone."

"Should we tell your brother and sister?" his dad asked.

"I would appreciate it, Dad. I don't want to talk to anyone. Uncle Dan is going to call Sarah's dad. I can't even do that. I know how hard he's going to take it."

After Tyler left, Alice and Ian broke down and spent the night comforting one another.

"I've never felt so helpless in my life. I want to go and bring her home but I don't know where to go to," said Alice crying.

"We all feel helpless, Alice. Poor John is going to be devastated when he hears."

Ian called Conor and Fiona. They were both in shock. Conor said he would call Kevin and he in turn would call his family.

"Conor, tell Kevin to make sure nobody from his family calls John before Uncle Dan does."

"I will make sure, Dad," Conor promised.

As he lay in bed alone Tyler was tormented by thoughts of what this abductor had in mind for her. He assumed it was a man and that his intensions were rape. Usually that followed with murder lest the victim identify her rapist. How swift would his moves be? Would he hold her up in some place for a while or would he do his dastardly deeds immediately? It had been about five hours now. Was she still alive even now? He felt bad that the last words he had with her were angry ones. He was angry because he was afraid that this would happen. "Dear God, please watch over her and bring her back safe to me."

He couldn't sleep so he got up and walked around the house. Wherever he went in the house, Sarah was there. In the dining room he remembered the wonderful time she had given him and his family at Christmas. He thought of how festive the table was and how exquisitely beautiful she looked sitting across from him; in the living room where they opened the presents that were under the fairy tale tree and he gave her the belated engagement ring and how happy she had been. He thought of how apologetic she was that she hadn't bought him very much when all he wanted was the happy day that she had provided; in the family room where the four of them sat and laughed and laughed on New Year's Eve and how she shared her story about the man sleeping in church. Nobody could provide him with the wonderful memories that Sarah had given him in the short time they had been together. In his bedroom he remembered their wedding night and how sweetly she gave herself to him. She was so innocent and yet willing to give all of herself to him without shame. That was how much she loved him and he knew it. He didn't believe that she could give herself to another man so freely. He even thought of the bad times when he was such a fool that he could have caused a breakup in the relationship. There was the time with that girl at the outdoor party. Sarah stood up for herself and put both the girl and him in their places. Then there was the time when she came back from France and he had confronted her with the notes. He still couldn't forgive himself for making her feel so insecure and hurt that time. The same person who had her now caused those bad times in their relationship.

After Tyler left to go home, Dan and his men had gone into the mall and questioned some of the sales people in the baby store Sarah had gone to. The girls certainly remembered her and answered the questions.

"No! There was no one with her. She was definitely alone," one of the girls said.

"She was only here a few minutes. She had asked us to wrap the gift and had paid for it over the phone with a credit card, so all she had to do was pick it up," another said. Dan asked a few more questions then thanked the girls and left the store. This was the worst experience in Dan's career. He sat in his office staring at the phone. She had not been heard from for a couple of hours now and Dan knew he couldn't put off calling John any longer. It was the first thing he had to do since leaving the mall. Other family members would be hearing about it and he wanted to make sure he was the one to break the news to John. He had experience, of course, letting loved ones know of a tragedy but when you are close to the people involved; it makes it a lot harder. The phone rang twice before Dan heard John's voice. "Hello!"

"John, Dan Rogers here. I'm afraid I have bad news," he knew he had to get straight to the point. "We are sure that Sarah has been abducted," he said as he waited for John's response. It didn't come for what seemed like ages. "Did you hear me John?"

"Yes. I'm just trying to understand. Who would want to hurt Sarah? It had to be a stranger. Everyone who knows her has to just love her," he hesitated knowing that he was babbling. "I'm sorry Dan. I just lost control of my mouth. When and how did it happen?"

Dan went on to tell John what they knew. "It doesn't sound good at all, Dan." Dan heard John cry. "What can I do?"

Dan told him there was nothing right now but that he may be questioning him and his wife later to see if they have anything that would help him and the department. "By the way John, Tyler didn't call you himself because he couldn't bring himself to tell you that your little girl had been stolen. He is a wreck right now. He wants to go get her but doesn't know what direction to go in".

"I know how he feels. I've never felt so helpless," John agreed.

Olivia was in the kitchen and didn't hear the conversation. "Olivia, please sit down. I have some bad news."

She slowly sat down while staring at John. *What could it be,* she thought? *Maybe he was finally going to ask for a divorce.*

She sat quietly waiting. "Sarah has been abducted."

She turned pale and just kept staring at him.

"Olivia?"

She started muttering. "We didn't take care of her. We let her go into the big wicked city all by herself and her husband couldn't protect her. I knew all along she should be here . . ."

"Stop Olivia!" her husband interrupted. "None of us is to blame for this. Sarah is living the life she wants."

"Living? Living? We don't even know that," Olivia almost screamed.

"Don't say that, Liv. We've got to hope."

Olivia kept muttering about how Sarah should have stayed at home and how they should never have allowed her to go. John really felt like she was blaming him since he was the one who encouraged her to go off to college. He tried to no avail to calm Olivia down. He was trying to deal with his own fear for his daughter. He couldn't listen to his wife any more. He grabbed his coat and walked to the door. Turning he called, "Come on Tweed."

He and Tweed went for a walk. It was a cold night. Enough to bring tears to a person's eyes but the tears running down John Kincaid's face was not because of the cold. He walked for quite a while until he found himself outside Kathleen's house. Kathleen saw him from the window and went out to bring him in.

"What has you this upset, John?"

When they were inside John told her everything. The tears were still running down his face and he was shaking. Kathleen walked him to the couch and sat him down then sat next to him and took his hand in hers. There were no words she could say to console him.

"We can only pray for her safety, John. I will certainly set time apart each day for her."

They sat there for a long time until both had cried themselves dry.

"Olivia keeps saying we should never have let her go to the big city. It makes me feel bad because I encouraged her to go."

"John, don't think like that. Things like this happen here in Marshallville too. Sarah followed her dream.

Whatever the outcome is, she did follow her dream. She got the job that she wanted and she married the man she had always wanted. We have to pray and have hope and faith," Kathleen said trying to encourage him.

"You're right as always, Kathleen. We can't focus on the negative. As far as we know she is still alive and we have to think positive that she'll come back to us."

"We can pray for wisdom for the police department."

"You're a good woman, Kathleen. I hope God answers your prayers."

"Many people will be praying for her, John. Not just me."

"I know I should go home to Olivia but I just feel so comfortable here with you, Kathleen. If only we had met a long time ago." She patted his head. He looked at his watch. It was almost eleven o'clock. "She has been missing about six hours now. I would like to be selfish and stay here but I better go home and see how Olivia's doing." She walked him to the door and he and Tweed walked back home.

Olivia was sitting staring at nothing in particular. She had a blank look on her face. John walked over and sat beside her.

"We could have both been better parents but Sarah loves us and she knows that we love her," he said trying to console her. They had never been in an emotional crisis like this and he was unsure of how to approach his wife.

"This is exactly what I was trying to protect her from. Maybe I went about it the wrong way but the only way I knew how was to keep her by my side," she said crying now. He had never seen Olivia cry before. It touched him.

"Every parent wants to keep their children close to them but they grow up and have to make their own lives. That's exactly what Sarah did. Who knows it could have happened even if she was still living in Marshallville."

"Who in Marshallville would want harm to come to Sarah?"

"I don't know, Olivia. I just know we have to keep our minds clear in case we can be of help. I am going to call my brother."

The next day Tyler went into the office to take care of some things but decided to cancel his appointments. He couldn't concentrate on anything but Sarah.

"Tyler, why don't you take some time off?" suggested Kevin. "You look exhausted."

"I didn't sleep. I don't know how I can sleep while she is out there in harm's way."

"You will be of more help if you're more alert," Kevin told him.

"I probably will take a nap later today. I go crazy sitting around doing nothing. I've never felt so helpless, Kevin" he said walking over to the window. It was a bleak day, which suited his mood. "I have absolutely no clue. She could be anywhere out there and I don't even know in what direction to head," he said staring outside. "All I have is a black car. I don't have the license plate number or anything."

"Did Dan come up with anything regarding Gloria's death and the fact that they both worked for the Canto modeling agency?"

"No! He didn't think the agency was a link. I think Gloria was just unlucky that night. I don't think the person was after Gloria. I think he had followed Sarah."

"I wish I had something to give you, Tyler. This guy has been so mysterious," said Kevin.

"I think I'll go and see Uncle Dan. I'll talk to you later."

"Sure!" Kevin said feeling very worried for both Sarah and Tyler. He was not sure what Tyler would do if Sarah did not return. Sarah was exactly the girl that Tyler had been looking for and now she was gone.

Dan was sitting with the notes in front of him when Tyler walked into his office.

"Do you have time for me?"

"Come in Tyler. I have been sitting looking over these notes that you gave me. The way they're written is like trying to make you think there was something between Sarah and the writer. Like I said before, he was definitely trying to drive a wedge between the two of you."

"It first started with him following Sarah in the black car, then the picture of Sarah and Sam going into a hotel room. I told you about that. That was the first time Sarah and I had a big fight and almost broke up, then came the notes and the phone calls. He probably followed her more times than we know. We're sure it was him that followed her to Gloria's house but she didn't see his car even though she said she had been looking for it."

"I don't want to alarm you, but we have another case of a missing girl from Austin. She lived close to Marshallville," said Uncle Dan showing a picture to Tyler. "Her name is Vanessa."

"When did she disappear?"

"A week ago," he answered.

"And she still has not been found?" asked Tyler with a note of discouragement.

"We are working all the angles. Don't get despondent on us. We'll have to touch base with you now and then and we need all the encouragement we can get," Dan admonished him.

John, Dan's partner walked in, "There are two other girls that disappeared last year that have never been found. They disappeared from Austin and guess where they're from?"

"Marshallville?" Dan guessed.

"Yep! At least one of them is, the other is close by in Johnson City."

"Did you pull their files?"

"Right here" he said throwing the files on Dan's desk. "There doesn't seem to be anything in common with Sarah."

"It would be hard to find anything in common with Sarah and any other girl when she was growing up. Her mother practically kept her as a prisoner. Except for going to school and working part time at the ice-cream parlor, she wasn't allowed to do anything else. She had no friends and her mother would not allow her to join any kind of association. She felt the need to keep control of Sarah. The only other thing was that she took Sarah every Sunday to this weird church in town. It was kind of like a cult."

"A cult?" Dan's ears picked up. "What was the name of the church?"

"It was a strange name. I think it was Church of the Chosen People, or something like that."

"John, see if you can find out if any of the other girls went to this church."

Tyler rang the doorbell and Mr. Kincaid answered. "Hello Tyler, come on in. Have you heard anything? It's been two days." Mr. Kincaid looked pale and tired. He kept looking at Tyler as though begging for something positive.

"Sorry, I haven't heard anything. John I would like to ask you and Mrs. Kincaid a few questions."

"Livia," John called to his wife. After she came and acknowledged Tyler her husband said, "Tyler would like to ask us a few questions." Tyler could tell that she was worried but he could also see a look of disdain on her face for him. She probably felt that he had failed to protect her daughter from this evil person.

"We will be happy to answer anything if it will help bring our daughter back," she said. He almost felt like she emphasized *our daughter*.

"Thank you Mrs. Kincaid. I know this is a hard time for you both but we have to pull together and do whatever we can," Tyler said almost apologetically for having to impose upon them at this difficult time.

"Go ahead, son," said John Kincaid.

"Has anyone made inquiries about Sarah since she moved to Austin, from either of you?"

"Well of course. Any time I run into Mr. Shannon from the ice-cream parlor he would ask how she was doing and I would usually just tell him she was doing well, enjoying her job, etc. Of course now everyone knows that she has disappeared and are worried, they want to know of any news."

"Before she disappeared, whenever he asked about her did he look for details?"

"No, just a polite inquiry." John Kincaid replied.

"What about you, Mrs. Kincaid?" Tyler asked.

"Some of the people at church inquire about her. Reverend Barker of course was very concerned about her and always made sure to find out how she was doing. You know, like making sure she was in a good neighborhood. He knows Austin so he would inquire into her whereabouts to make sure that she was safe and that she had a job to take care of herself. He was her pastor all her growing years, after all. He is extremely worried about her now."

"Yes, of course" Tyler answered. "Does he happen to drive a black car?"

"The only vehicle I have seen him with is a red truck. I never wanted her to leave in the first place. I knew that she would get in trouble going to that big city and dressing like she did."

"Sarah didn't do anything to deserve this, Mrs. Kincaid," Tyler said trying not to show his anger.

"Of course not." John Kincaid agreed. "My daughter is a very good person."

"Yes, she is" Tyler said then thought *I hope she still is and not was.*

Olivia Kincaid knew she had blown it again. She was always outside of the loop when it came to Sarah.

"Well I'm just trying to find out any information I can. Thank you. I will be sure and keep in touch with you, John."

"Thank you, Tyler for all you're doing to help find Sarah. If there is anything I can do let me know. I can't tell you how devastated I feel. But I know you feel the same way," John Kincaid said as he reached out to shake Tyler's hand.

Tyler came back to see Dan. "I talked with the Kincaids. Not too much information there, except Mrs. Kincaid seems to give quite a bit of information to her pastor about where Sarah is working and where she stays. I also remember on New Year's Day when Sarah called her parents, her mother indicated how worried she was all the time about her flying so much. She said the pastor prayed for her every time she flew, so he must have known her schedule, somewhat. Of course, like her mother said, he was her childhood pastor."

"That's interesting, however the Sheriff's department in Marshallville have been watching him and said there is no sign of suspicious behavior. He lives next door to the church so he walks to it. No sign of a black car. The only vehicle they have seen him drive is a red pickup truck."

"That's what Mrs. Kincaid said," Tyler remarked sitting back in the chair thinking. *Red truck, red truck didn't Sarah say something about a red truck. When did she say that and what were the circumstances?*

"What's going on in your head, Tyler?" Dan asked as he was looking through the notes again.

"I'm trying to think. Sarah mentioned one time about a red truck but I can't remember why she mentioned it."

John walked in. "All the girls had attended that church at one time. All of them left for Austin around the same age as Sarah was when she left. Probably as soon as they graduated from high school they either went to college or took a better paying job in the big city. It took a while to get all the information since a couple of the parents were hard to get a hold of. Only Sarah's mother attends the church now. The parents of the two girls that disappeared last year have moved away from the area and Vanessa's mother stopped going about a year ago."

Tyler still couldn't stop thinking about the red truck. Suddenly he jumped out of his chair. "I've got it," Tyler yelled.

"What? What is it, son?" Dan inquired anxiously.

"After we left your office that day when you were questioning Sarah about Gloria, she felt bad because she believed she had led the killer to Gloria's apartment," he was talking so fast with excitement.

"Calm down a bit son, so we can follow you," Dan said.

"Okay! I asked her if she saw the black car and she said there was a red truck behind her and she couldn't see what was behind it. A red truck was behind her the night of Gloria's murder."

"Didn't the clerk at Gloria's apartment house say that while he was outside taking care of Gloria, a truck drove past?" John the deputy asked.

"It could all be a coincidence, but it is something, especially knowing that all the girls went to his church. John, call the Sheriff and let him know this information."

"Can we trust everyone in the Sheriff's office?" Tyler questioned. "I mean what if someone is a member of the church? I don't want anything to go wrong."

"Me neither, son, but they are closer than we are. At least they can keep watch."

CHAPTER 27

She was feeling groggy as she started to revive from the ether. Her stomach was very upset. She knew she was going to throw up and would like to find a bathroom but she had no idea where she was. She was in a dank, dark room that she was not familiar with. She moaned since not only was her stomach turning, but her head felt like there was a ton of bricks sitting on it.

"Are you alright?" a young woman's voice inquired.

Sarah was trying to figure out what was going on before responding to this voice.

"Are you okay?" the voice asked again coming closer to her. Sarah could see her vaguely. She was about her age.

"I'm going to be sick. Is there a bathroom?"

"Let me help you," the voice said as she reached out to help Sarah to her feet. She led her to a room and showed her where the toilet was. Sarah fell to her knees and threw up into the toilet. She couldn't even see if it was clean or not but at this moment all she wanted to do was to relieve herself of what was causing her problem. After throwing up she felt better. Even her head felt better. She started to get herself together and allowed the voice to guide her out of the bathroom back to the room. She sat down.

"Who are you?" she asked the voice.

"My name is Vanessa. I knew you a little bit when we both attended this church. I left almost three years ago and moved to Austin to get a better job."

"What church and how do you know who I am? I can hardly see you," Sarah inquired.

"He told me your name and like I said, I sort of remember you. This is the Church of the Chosen People."

"What are we doing here and who brought us here?" asked a confused Sarah.

"Reverend Barker is our abductor. He said that his calling was to purify us with his holy seed so we would get into heaven," Vanessa told her. "He said we have the impure seed in us because our husbands are not a part of this church. I always thought he was weird but not this weird. He is evil."

"Is he talking about raping us?"

"Yes! Three times each. Then he said we would be pure and go to heaven," Vanessa said angrily. "He has already raped me twice."

"Evil is not the word," said Sarah finding it hard to believe her ears. "He is the devil incarnate," she said angrily. At first she was stunned but now she was very angry.

"My mother used to be a member of this church. She stopped attending last year," Vanessa told Sarah.

"Mine still attends," said Sarah wondering what her mom would think of it now. This will be devastating for her. "What do you think he has in mind for us after raping us three times? Surely he will not let us go? He should know that we would go to the police."

"He hasn't given me any clues," Vanessa answered.

"Is there any possibility of getting out of here?" Sarah asked.

"He locks the door from the outside," Vanessa replied.

"We'll have to try and think of a way," Sarah suggested. "Otherwise, it doesn't look good for us."

"I have already checked around for some kind of weapon, but there's nothing here."

"But there are two of us and only one of him," said Sarah trying to encourage Vanessa.

"We could rush him and kick him in the shins. That might bring him to his knees."

"With two of us, we might be able to subdue him somehow. There was no way for me to do it alone," Vanessa admitted. "Meanwhile, good luck trying to sleep on these hard benches."

"I still feel sleepy from whatever he put me out with. I haven't eaten since noon today. Is there anything around here worth eating?" Sarah asked.

"No! He brings in some cheese and crackers and not very much of that. I'm sorry. I ate every bit of it."

"That's okay."

The next morning the door opened and Sarah saw him. She recognized his stubby little body. He turned the dimmer up slightly and Sarah saw him a lot better. She had never liked him and now he disgusted her. "Well, well Sarah, we finally have you," he said leering at her. "You tried to trick me a couple of times but I knew I would get you back in the sanctuary."

"Sanctuary? You mean this dark hell hole."

"Careful Sarah," cautioned Vanessa. "He's mean."

"Be prepared for your first cleansing this afternoon Sarah." Then he went back out again.

That afternoon, Barker came back to give Sarah her first cleansing. He locked Vanessa in the bathroom so that she couldn't interfere. As he came toward Sarah, she screamed at him. "I don't want your evil, dirty body near me."

He slapped her hard and she fell to the ground. He bent over her and hit her again. Her head crashed on the floor. It knocked her out for a few moments. Sarah's mind was a blur partially from him hitting her and partially because of the shock of this disgusting, evil man violating her in one of the most brutal, horrific ways. She felt panicky as she tried pushing him off to no avail. He was much too heavy. She scratched his face trying to get to his eyes, but he hit her again. After he was finished he got up, opened the bathroom door and let Vanessa out.

"Take care of her," he said and walked out locking the door and dimming the light.

Tyler had rented a hotel room across from the church. It wasn't a large church but it wasn't very small either. He wasn't sure what he was looking for but Mrs. Kincaid's statement of the inquiries that Barker made of Sarah had him slightly suspicious. The fact that the girls all had gone to that church at one time or another also made him suspicious, but the red truck was the cincher. Especially because a red truck was behind Sarah on the night of Gloria's murder. He looked up and down the street from the room window. The street was very quiet. The parsonage lights were out indicating that no one was home. He decided to take a walk and maybe check the church out. He didn't see any car around that would indicate the sheriff's boys were there. Just as he stepped out of the hotel, a black car pulled into the garage of the parsonage. A few minutes later the driver of the black car drove out with the red truck and parked at the back of the church.

"You scumbag, you're mine." He knew he couldn't go after Barker just yet. He had to make sure Sarah was safe, if she was even alive. *She has to be, she just has to be,* he thought. Tyler knew somehow he had to get inside before Barker left.

He cautiously crossed the street and walked to the back. The truck was there, of course. Barker didn't know what Tyler looked like; at least he didn't think so. If he were to get caught he could make up a story about being interested in the church or just punch him and pretend to be a robber. Anything! Just so long as he got inside. He walked to the door. It was open.

Sarah and Vanessa heard him turn the key. Just being in his presence made them both feel sick.

He walked over to grab Vanessa's arm and both girls knew that he would attempt to lock her up in the bathroom again. "Don't let him do it, Vanessa," Sarah said running towards him. They both started kicking and punching him as hard as they could. He knocked Vanessa down then threw Sarah away from him. He then backed up to the door.

"I'm going to my cabin to fish while you two whores sit here and contemplate your sins. You have become an abomination to God. The two people responsible for your fall from grace Sarah is that over-sexed deviate you call a husband and that nigger whore. Good riddance to her."

"You murdered her, you evil, demonic monster. You will burn in hell for that," she said with more anger than she had ever felt. Neither had she ever felt so much hatred for anyone in her life.

"She was a nigger," he spat out the words.

"She was a beautiful black woman and you are an evil white man," she said moving towards him.

"You blasphemer," he said drawing the back of his hand across her face making her lip bleed. Her face was already bruised from the previous beating but it didn't make her stop.

"Tell me Barker, is being *evil* better than being *black* or is being *white* better than being a *beautiful spirit?* You don't know the teachings of Christ. Just who is your God, Barker? Beelzebub?"

He was furious. "How dare you talk to the Holy Servant of God like that." He slapped her again this time with more fury that knocked her to the floor. Vanessa watched fearfully. She wished Sarah would stop talking. She was afraid he would kill her. She didn't move. She was afraid of making him anymore angrier than he already was. But Sarah had unleashed her fury and couldn't stop. "There's nothing holy about murder or rape. As for being a servant of God, you are the servant of everything evil. You're a servant of your own lust, a servant of . . ."

He slapped her again. "You are going to die and go to hell! I will make sure of it."

"Oh yeah, Barker, we are shaking in our boots. Like God would listen to a devil like you," Sarah spat out the words. Barker stood over her.

"Leave her alone," Vanessa called out. "She's pregnant."

Sarah wished that Vanessa hadn't said that. He stood over her with fists clenched so tight his knuckles were white and with such fury in his face it was purple. His eyes were wild. She started to get up, but he took his hard booted foot and kicked her as hard as he could in the stomach. Not once but twice. She screamed.

"Bastard child," he said as he left and locked the door.

Tyler stealthily turned the handle and looked around. He didn't see anyone. *So far, so good,* he thought. He was looking around for a place to hide in case he needed it, when he heard a woman scream. He walked in the direction of her voice. There was a small corridor with only one door. Because the voice sounded muffled he assumed that the door might lead to a basement. He was about to try the handle when he heard a door slam shut then get locked. He heard footsteps ascending the stairs so he ran back. The only place he could find to hide was under a huge desk. He thought if Barker was to sit down at this desk he would most likely find him. He didn't care. If he did find him he would take him out anyway. He knew there was a woman down there and she had been hurt. Barker walked towards the desk and opened the drawer. He was mumbling but Tyler couldn't understand what he was saying. He heard him throw what sounded like a key in the drawer. He knew it was probably the one for the door. To Tyler's disappointment, Barker locked the drawer. He could tell by his mumbling, his loud stomping and throwing things that he was angry. After a while he walked to the back door and left.

Tyler waited a little while until he knew for sure that he had left. He saw the headlights leave the parking lot. He got up and went to try the door at the top of the stairs. It was locked. The sun had already set and it was a little dark in the office. He had brought a flashlight with him because he didn't want to have lights on in the church which might draw attention should someone be around. He tried the desk to make sure, but of course it was locked, just like he thought. He looked around for a screwdriver or something. Usually desks were easy to break into. He found a letter opener on the desk. It was cluttered, but Tyler's eyes fell on a Photoshop box and he remembered Sarah said that a program such as Photoshop had been used to alter the picture of her and Sam. He didn't take time to contemplate that. He had more important things to think about. It didn't take Tyler long to pry the desk open. There were a few keys in the desk. He took the one that looked like a door key and tried it. It worked. He walked down the stairs and at the bottom was one more door. He tried it but it was locked also just as he thought it would be. He kept praying that the scream he heard came from Sarah. He would rather she be hurt than dead. Vanessa heard someone try the door. "Sarah, I think he has come back." Sarah couldn't hear her. She had fallen into unconsciousness.

Tyler looked around. There had to be a key somewhere. He used his flashlight but it was so dark so he felt along the walls but didn't find anything. He ran back upstairs and hurried over to the desk. He heard a car outside. He turned off his flashlight and got under the desk again. He cowered down as much as he could and tried not to breathe too hard. He was worried because the desk had been broken into and he left the door at the top of the stairs open. The back door opened, then he heard it get locked, then closed. *He forgot to lock the door,* Tyler thought relieved. He left again. After Tyler was sure he was gone he got out from under the desk and grabbed the rest of the keys and ran back to the room in the basement. The first key he tried unlocked the door.

It was very dim inside. He could see the form of a woman kneeling on the floor. It looked like she was holding someone in her arms. Vanessa could tell by the form it wasn't Barker. This person was much taller and definitely not fat.

"Who are you?" the woman asked. Her voice was weak and it was obvious she was very upset and scared. He was disappointed that it wasn't Sarah's voice.

"My name is Tyler MacAulay. I'm looking for Sarah Kincaid MacAulay."

"Why are you looking for her?" Vanessa asked, being cautious of this stranger.

"I am her husband." Vanessa knew Sarah's husband's name was Tyler but she wanted to make sure.

"There is a dimmer switch outside to the right of the door, you can turn it up."

Tyler turned up the switch and went back inside. He saw that the person lying on the floor was Sarah. She was absolutely still. As he fell to his knees beside her he saw the blood.

"My God, what happened?" He felt her pulse and was grateful that she was still alive.

"He beat her," Vanessa was crying by now, "and before he left he kicked her in the stomach. She may have lost her baby," Vanessa told him.

"She's pregnant?" Tyler didn't wait for an answer. He pulled out his cell phone and dialed 9–1–1. "We need an ambulance sent immediately to the Church of the Chosen People on Main Street. Come to the back of the church. I will answer questions later. We have a pregnant girl that was beaten and is hemorrhaging. She has also lost consciousness." He then dialed his Uncle Dan on his cell phone.

"Uncle Dan, I have found Sarah. She is at the church just as we thought. Barker is not here. The other girl Vanessa is here and looks fine. Sarah is in pretty bad shape though. I have called for an ambulance," Tyler said hurriedly.

"I'll call the sheriff in Marshallville and inform him," Dan said. "I am heading that way now. I should be there in about forty-five minutes." Tyler hung up his phone and went back to attending Sarah.

"Sarah, please open your eyes," he said in desperation.

"John," Dan called from his office. John hurried in. He could tell by Dan's voice there was an emergency.

"Tyler has found Sarah and Vanessa. Grab the folder. I will call both sets of parents from the car." While John went to get the folder on the girls, Dan made a quick call to the sheriff.

The sheriff arrived at the same time as the ambulance. The ambulance men put Sarah very carefully onto the stretcher and covered her bruised and bloody body. The sheriff told them to take Vanessa also and have her checked out. Tyler rode with the sheriff and his deputy to the hospital. After about an hour Vanessa was discharged and the sheriff took her back to his office. He told Tyler that he wanted him there in an hour. Dan Rogers and Vanessa's parents and Sarah's parents would be there. He wanted to get Vanessa's statement before sharing with the parents of both girls.

When John Kincaid got the call from Dan he got so emotional he could hardly talk. "We'll go right to the sheriff's office. Thank you Dan." His voice was so shaky. He was trying not to cry. Seeing he was obviously very emotional Olivia asked, "What is it John?" She was afraid to hear the news thinking it was bad.

"They've found Sarah," he said with tears in his eyes.

Olivia put her hand up to her mouth and gave a gasp. Her eyes had the look of sheer terror in them.

"No, dear. Sarah is alive. She is hurt, but she is alive." Olivia actually ran into John's arms and both of them cried and laughed at the same time. "Is she okay?" she asked.

"I don't know. She's in the hospital. The other girl will be at the sheriff's office when we get there. We'll find out everything then. Get your coat."

When Tyler was able to go in and see Sarah he was very concerned. She had tubes going up her nose and in her arms and her face was badly bruised. She was still unconscious. He couldn't help thinking what would have happened if he hadn't gotten to her when he did. The doctor walked in.

"Is she going to be okay, doctor?" Tyler asked.

"She will be fine. She'll be in a lot of pain for a while. I will give you a prescription to get her some medication." If he ever got his hands on Barker, he was sure he would kill him. The longer he looked at Sarah and pictured Barker beating and kicking her the more outraged he became. "How dare he even touch her," he said aloud as he stared out the window wondering where Barker was. If he had any idea he would go after him, he decided. He had never had any notion of killing someone before but at this moment he was sure he would have no problem with killing Barker. He heard a moan behind him. He ran over to the bed. "Sarah darling I'm here." She was hurting really bad. Tyler went out to get a nurse who came and gave her a shot for the pain.

"She will get sleepy in a short while," the nurse informed him.

"Okay," then turning to Sarah "sweetheart, I will stay with you until you go to sleep and then I have to go to the sheriff's office, but I will be back when I am through there," he promised her.

She nodded and smiled at him. "How did I get here? I mean, how was I rescued?"

Tyler told her and assured her that Vanessa was okay. She was getting very sleepy and just before dozing off she murmured "My hero." The sheriff put one of his men outside her hospital room.

John and Olivia arrived before Vanessa's parents. When Alan and Kay Smith came in and saw their daughter they both ran over to hug her. All three of them broke down crying. Dan motioned the rest of the people to leave and let them have a little time alone. John and Olivia certainly knew what the Smiths were feeling.

By the time Tyler arrived at the sheriff's office, everyone was there. They were waiting for him before starting.

"First of all, I would like to thank the Sheriff and his office for their complete cooperation with the Austin Police Department. I would also like to thank Tyler

MacAulay for his endless search for clues that helped lead us to Sarah and Vanessa. In fact, at times he drove me crazy but it was because of his persistence that we were able to start putting two and two together," Dan Rogers said then paused and smiled and nodded to Tyler and the Sheriff. Everyone clapped and thanked the Sheriff and Tyler for their work.

"Vanessa gave the Sheriff and I her statement. We will get Sarah's later. She is in the hospital."

"Is she going to be okay?" Mr. Kincaid asked anxiously. Dan turned to Tyler questioningly.

"She was unconscious but she woke up just before I left. The doctor said she would be okay."

"Thank you, her mom and I will be eternally grateful," John said smiling appreciatively at Tyler. Olivia just gave him a polite nod of her head.

Dan started to read. "Vanessa disappeared on Monday, January 11 while walking in her neighborhood. Sarah disappeared while returning to her car after shopping at a mall on Monday, January 18. Both girls had an ether-soaked cloth forced to their face, and taken to a dimly lit room. They both knew their abductor." Dan continued. This caused everyone to look up at him questioningly. "I will ask Vanessa to give a short statement as to what happened from that time," Dan continued then nodded to Vanessa. The fact that they knew their abductor had them all concerned. She was very nervous because she knew what a shock it was going to be to both sets of parents when they found out who he was. She wished Sarah was there with her.

"When I woke up I was in a room so dimly lit that I couldn't see my surroundings. I had no idea where I was."

Everyone was listening intently. "After a short while the door opened and a man came in. I couldn't make him out but I sort of knew the voice. He told me unless he put his holy seed in me I would go to hell." Olivia Kincaid looked at her inquisitively. "The next time he came in he told me it was time for my cleansing. He pulled me to the floor and raped me." Kay Smith put her hands over her face and let out a little cry. "While he was on top of me I got a better look at him. I recognized him as Reverend Barker."

Olivia cried out "You must be mistaken. It might have been a custodian. You said it was dim in the room."

"I am not mistaken, Mrs. Kincaid. He raped me two more times after that."

Alan Smith put his arm around his daughter. Like John and Tyler he felt anger not only at Barker, but also at himself for not being able to have protected his daughter from this atrocity.

"About a week or so later, he came in carrying another girl. I found out it was Sarah. We didn't recognize one another because we have both changed our appearance so much and we didn't really know each other very well as children but he told me who she was." Olivia was getting restless. This whole situation was making her uncomfortable. If in fact Reverend Barker had committed this hideous crime, then she was the one that had put Sarah in harm's way. She was having a hard time accepting the accusation.

"He came in the day after Sarah arrived and said the same thing to her. He said she had pagan seed in her, meaning Tyler's, and that only the seed of the Holy Servant of God, meaning his, could cleanse her and keep her from going to hell. She told *him* to go to hell. He hit her across the face." John Kincaid was silently listening but his face was livid.

"The next time he came in, he locked me in the bathroom and he raped her."

John jumped out of his chair. He turned to his wife, "All this time you have been criticizing Sarah calling her a jezebel because she wouldn't follow that murdering rapist's teaching. I'm going to burn that freaking church down and after that I am going to hunt him down and butcher him and throw him in the woods for the wild animals to devour."

"John, please don't say anything. I know these are just words of anger, but don't say them, please," Dan pleaded with John. Tyler sat the whole time with a tense jaw. He was so angry but his uncle had told him to try and keep it together because he knew he was going to have to deal with the families. He put his hand on John's shoulder letting him know that he felt exactly the same way. John looked up into Tyler's face. Tyler had never seen him look so full of hate. John Kincaid loved his baby girl, as he liked to call her, and having this happen to her was more than he could endure. At this moment, John almost hated his wife, but he couldn't just blame her. He knew that he should have stepped in a lot more to shelter Sarah from the life that she was forced to live during her growing up years. It was a life that she hated. Listening to Vanessa, Tyler started to understand what the notes meant. *He would take care of everything. She would be in heaven.*

"He released me from the bathroom," Vanessa continued, "I could tell that he had badly beaten her, but I could also tell that she had put up a fight because his face had scratches all over it. She was almost unconscious. He told me to take care of her and left." She stopped to take a drink of water. Her throat was so dry. She knew what she was saying was a shock to both sets of parents but she had to go on.

"When he came back today, he tried to rape her again. As he was coming towards me to grab my arm to put me in the bathroom, Sarah rushed at him yelling for me to help fight him. We kicked and punched and he backed off. He called Gloria a nigger whore and Sarah called him an evil white man. He was furious. And during the argument he confessed to killing her friend, Gloria." Both Dan and the sheriff turned sharply towards her then looked at each other. John threw his head back, closed his eyes and took a deep breath.

"Sarah was furious and kept calling him evil names. I kept hoping she would be quiet but it was as if she couldn't stop. He hit her again but harder this time knocking her to the ground," Vanessa continued. "He was standing over her with such anger that his face was purple. I panicked and yelled out 'leave her alone, she's pregnant.' John Kincaid looked at Vanessa concernedly but Olivia just kept staring at the table in front of her, her jaw was tight and her face was ashen.

"When I called this out, he got more furious. The next thing I knew he kicked her hard in the stomach, two times. He was wearing heavy boots. After he left, I went over to try and help her. She told me she thought she was losing the baby and then she started to pass out. Shortly after that, Tyler came but by that time, she was unconscious."

"He killed our grandbaby," John said looking at his wife. Olivia could not look at anyone. She was having her own battle going on. She barely heard her husband. So many, many thoughts were hammering at her. *Almost twenty years I believed this man. I exposed him to my child and he ended up raping her and killing her baby. How can I forgive myself for this?* She looked like she was in shock. Then John looked up at Tyler who was still standing near him.

"You were the one who rescued them?" John asked Tyler.

Dan answered. "Yes, he did. Even though he took it upon himself, we are thankful he found the girls. But don't do anything like that again Tyler," he said scolding him in a teasing manner.

Dan then turned to Vanessa. "Did he say anything that would give you a clue as to where he was going?" Dan asked.

"Only that he was going to his cabin to fish."

Kay Smith's face was pale. "I can't believe I could have been taken in by someone capable of such evil behavior. I believed him." Her husband put one arm around his wife, the other around his daughter.

Vanessa was glad that the meeting was over. Her father hugged her and apologized profusely for not being more protective of her.

John Kincaid could hardly get out of his chair. He was stunned. Olivia stood up, straightened out her clothes and walked over to Tyler in a perfunctory manner and said,"Thank you Tyler for caring about our daughter. Now I would like to see her."

When they arrived at her hospital room, Olivia was surprised to see a guard outside. This could only mean that the sheriff felt her life was still in danger.

She was sitting up, and except for the mess her face was in, she looked pretty good. John almost ran to her and put his arms around her gently. "I want to give you a big hug but I know you're in a lot pain. I'm just so thankful and grateful to everyone who helped. Especially Tyler."

"I'm thankful also to be able to see you all again. That was my worst thought. That I would never see you all again." Then she turned to Tyler. "The doctor said I could go home tomorrow. He will give me some pain pills to help me, until the pain goes away" she said smiling at Tyler. "I can't wait to go home. It seems like it has been months."

Olivia felt a little tug at her heart. She still wished she had Sarah at home with her, but she knew this was best for her.

"Sarah, I can't tell you how sorry I am about what happened. I feel very guilty for having brought this man into your life and putting you in danger," her mother said very sincerely but still with not very much emotion. It was the first time that Olivia had been able to say exactly what she felt. The guilt and embarrassment held her back from completely letting go. She was embarrassed by the fact that she had harassed Sarah for not following his teachings and calling her names because she chose to look more modern.

"Momma," Sarah said reaching out her hands to her mom. "It was not your fault. He had you, as well as the rest of the congregation, fooled. He seems to think he is God." Olivia reached out and hugged her. Sarah knew how difficult it was for her mother but she held back the tears. She was glad she didn't have to be in the room when she was told that Barker had violated her daughter. Everyone felt awkward. This was a big confession for Olivia. No one knew what to say.

"I'm not sure that I will ever let you step outside of the house alone again," Tyler came to the rescue.

The sheriff and Uncle Dan arrived to talk with Sarah. They were quick since they already had the facts from Vanessa. They just confirmed them with her.

When he got back to the hotel, he took the time to call his parents and Kevin and let them know they had found her.

"Thank God she's safe Tyler and thanks for letting me know she is going to be okay. What a relief, " Kevin said. "I know you have other people to call so I'll talk to you when you get back here. Meanwhile I'll call my family and let them know."

"Hello," Ian MacAulay said into the phone, wondering who would be calling them so late.

"Dad, it's Tyler. We have found Sarah. She's in the hospital but will be going home tomorrow. We will explain everything to you later. Tell Mom that I will call her tomorrow."

Ian couldn't get his voice he had a lump in his throat and was trying not to let his son know he was crying.

"Dad?"

"I'm just overcome with emotion right now," Ian said breaking up. "I will let your mom know. Please do call us tomorrow as soon as you get home. We'll want to see Sarah as soon as possible."

Alice was curious as to who was calling at eleven o'clock at night. She was in her pajamas when she walked into the room to find her husband sitting on the couch crying.

"Ian," Alice said with terror in her eyes and her right hand over her heart. "What's wrong?" She was afraid of the answer because she thought he might be crying because they found Sarah's body.

He looked at her with tears running down his face but he was smiling. "Sarah is with Tyler. She will be home tomorrow, Alice."

"Oh, thank God."

Once more they wrapped arms around each other and cried, but this time with relief.

CHAPTER 28

It was about four o'clock when they got home. She was released around ten in the morning and Olivia Kincaid had actually invited them to lunch. In spite of all the pain and suffering, this was really a happy moment for Sarah. Tyler and her dad sat on the back porch talking about fishing and horses before lunch was served. She would love to have helped her mom but she was still quite weak and her mom insisted she sit down and rest. It was the first time she actually felt like they were a real family. Her momma had put together a wonderful lunch. Cooking was one of her specialties. She learned through her husband how Sarah had come to enjoy seafood salad since she moved to Austin, so she put together the best Sarah had ever had. The air was a little tense but her mom was really trying and she appreciated it. She even came from the kitchen carrying the cake stand that Tyler had bought her. "It is lovely, Momma. This is the first time I have seen it. Thank you for showing it to me."

As Tyler helped her out of the car, Sarah stood looking at the house. "It has never looked as welcoming as it does right now. I love this place, even more now." He helped her over to the couch and sat next to her pulling her close to him. They sat silently for a while then Sarah said, "I wasn't sure I would ever see you again. In fact I was sure I wouldn't. Barker had threatened to put me away if I caused any more trouble."

"Someone is going to put him away."

"What do you mean Tyler?" she said with concern.

"Oh, I'm just talking honey, but between Alan Smith, your dad and me, anyone of us is capable."

"Well, I hope none of you get such a notion. It would be devastating for Vanessa, her mom, my mom and me if any of you would end up in prison because of him. Let the law take care of him. They know he will be back for Sunday service. They will get him," Sarah pleaded.

"Like I said Sarah, I was just talking. Would you like to go to bed?"

"I am very tired but I want to enjoy being home with you. I want to stay up as long as I can. I would like to get back to a normal sleep schedule as soon as possible and to be honest, I'm afraid to go to sleep. I'm afraid of dreams and afraid of wakening up to find myself back in that dark room."

"I will keep my arms around you all night and if you wake up from a bad dream, you will know I am right there."

She was quiet for a while then said, "Tyler I know it wasn't my fault, but I am sorry about the rape. I always wanted you to be the only man."

He took her face in his hands and turned it towards him and looked her straight in the eyes. "Baby he raped you. You gave yourself to me. That is the difference. I am still the only man you have given yourself to and I appreciate you very much."

She fell asleep within a short time, due partially to the medication and he carried her to the bedroom and laid her on top of the bed. She slept for an hour or so then got up and had something to eat but by nine o'clock she was tired and went back to bed.

Sarah was surprised at how well she had slept. Actually she was so exhausted that she slept ten hours. Tyler was happy to let her sleep fourteen hours if she needed it. She looked so much better this morning.

"Did you have any bad dreams?"

"I don't think I had any dreams. I think I was unconscious all night."

"When I called Mom yesterday afternoon, she said she would like to come over and help around the house. I told her I would talk to you. If you don't want anyone around, we all understand."

"Maybe instead of her coming over here, we can take a drive over to her house. I would like an opportunity to be out in the fresh air, but I want to be able to come back here whenever we want and just be by ourselves. Do you understand what I mean?"

"I think that's a great idea and none of us wants to wear you out. We all want you back on your feet as soon as possible. I made some coffee. Would you like some?"

She nodded yes. He handed her a cup and sat down next to her. "Sarah, why didn't you tell me about the baby?"

"I am so sorry about losing the baby. It has been hard for me to talk about it. I had just found out about the baby two weeks ago but I couldn't bring myself to tell you about it because of my feelings. Forgive me for being self-ish Tyler, but I didn't think I wanted anyone to come into our lives right now. I have been soaking in all the attention and love that you give me and I didn't want to share it. Not now. At the same time, I felt thrilled to be carrying your baby inside of me. I was torn with mixed emotions and when I felt the baby leave my body, I was ashamed of myself." By this time tears were coming down her face.

Putting his hands on her shoulders he turned her to face him. He looked straight into her eyes. "Don't feel ashamed, Sarah. You didn't do anything wrong. The pregnancy was an accident. Neither of us was ready for it. Your feelings were not malicious. We'll have a family after we've been married a while." They held on to one another for a long time allowing their emotions to be free.

Sarah called home but no one answered. She didn't leave a message on the machine. She decided to call later. "Would you help me take a bath? It is still hard for me to move around and I'm afraid I will fall into the tub."

"Sure! Just stay seated until I get your bath ready." He filled the tub with water and some of her favorite aromatherapy oil. He helped her take off her clothes. He gasped when he saw her body. Her ribs were totally black and blue. He hadn't seen it last night when he undressed her because he did not put the light in the room on. He held back a sob and instead punched his fist into the wall. It startled Sarah. She wasn't sure what was happening to him. "Tyler?"

He turned and saw her frightened look. "I'm sorry baby, I hate him so much for what he has done to you," he said putting his arms around her. He helped her into the tub and sponged her ever so tenderly.

Alice and Ian MacAulay were so excited to see Sarah. Alice threw her arms around her and burst out crying. "Oh my sweet, sweet Sarah. I have to tell you I didn't think I would ever see you again, even though I didn't admit it to anyone," she said wiping her eyes and cheeks with her handkerchief.

"I think most of us had our doubts Sarah," Ian confessed while giving her a huge hug. Tyler saw her grimace.

"Dad you can't hug her so tight. Her ribs are bruised badly."

"Oh dear! I'm sorry but this is such a relief Sarah. To have you with us, when we were thinking the worst, is a miracle to us," Ian said with a lot of emotion.

Sarah was thrilled to have so many people caring about her. She put her arm through Tyler's and smiling up at him she said, "Thanks to my big hero."

"Come on in and sit down. What did Tyler have to do with it?" Ian asked.

Tyler and Sarah sat down on the couch. Ian and Alice had their favorite chairs and everyone knew not to sit in them. Not that they would say anything but the family knew they were just very comfortable with their chairs.

"Now tell us what you mean, Sarah?" Ian asked again.

Sarah told them how Tyler was the one that saved her and Vanessa.

"Actually, Uncle Dan and the sheriff were right behind me, so if I didn't find them, they would have."

"Although, Uncle Dan told me that Tyler gave them many clues that led to the suspicion of Barker," piped in Sarah. "I think his uncle was very proud of him."

"We're not only proud of him but thank him for bringing you back to us," declared Ian MacAulay.

"Sarah, I have never seen my son so devastated than he was the night you disappeared. His dad and I had no idea how to console him," said Alice. "There was just nothing in this world that could except having you back."

"That was what really bothered me. I knew he would be frantic as well as the rest of my family and friends and I wasn't sure that I would get back. In fact, I thought my life was over."

Alice started to cry again. Tyler and Sarah knew it would be a very emotional time for his parents and really did not want to share too many details but knew that they would get it all from the news so they felt obligated to have it come from them. Like the other men, Ian MacAulay was outraged when he heard about the beatings she had endured. The rape had both of them furious but when they heard about their unborn grandchild, they were horrified. They talked about John Kincaid's fury and Ian said he could completely understand. He would like to kill the diabolical fiend and give him to the buzzards also.

"Conor and his family are out of town, but they were so relieved to hear that you were back with us and Fiona said she would call you later. She thought maybe we would like to be alone with you both for a little while and she was right," Alice said almost apologetically. "But I told both she and Conor that as soon as you got a little stronger we will all get together here. Your parents too."

"Talking about getting stronger, I think she needs to get back home and rest for a while," Tyler said. Alice and Ian understood. They were so happy to see Tyler looking like his own self again.

They all walked to the door and said their goodbyes. Tyler spoke alone to his dad before he left, "Dad could you give the details to Fiona and Conor. I don't want Sarah to have to relive this over and over but I wouldn't want them getting it from the news."

"Don't worry son, your mom and I will take care of it."

CHAPTER 29

The driver of the car knew his cabin was somewhere in the area. The driver was determined to drive around until the red truck was found. It took almost an hour but there it was. The garage door was open and the truck outside had a little Jon boat on the bed. The car pulled over and parked a little beyond his house and the driver walked back towards the garage and watched very quietly at the man's back as he casually and methodically chose his bait and rod. There didn't seem to be a caring or nervous bone in his body. He picked up his tackle box and rod and turned to go towards the truck. A look of shock came over his face.

"Olivia, I'm surprised to see you here," he said nervously.

"I just thought you'd like to hear that the Sheriff found my daughter," Olivia said in a cold, flat voice.

He tried to look surprised. "Well that is just great, Olivia. Where was she?"

"In the basement of your church. We all sat and listened to Vanessa tell the Sheriff how you abducted them and raped them and killed Sarah's baby."

He hesitated trying to find the right words. Olivia was a parishioner. Perhaps he could make her understand.

"Olivia, both those girls were going to hell. I was saving them by cleansing them."

"So when rape is being committed by you it is called a cleansing?"

"Only by my seed. I am the holy servant of God."

"What about the innocent child?" asked Olivia.

"It was a bastard."

"It was my grandchild. I don't want to hear your lies anymore and I'm not going to have my daughter dragged through the court system. I will not have some sleazy lawyer bring disgrace to her. The only way I know how to avoid that from happening is to not have a trial. We can't have a trial if we don't have a suspect, can we?"

"What are you saying, Olivia?" *Was she giving him a chance to get away?* he wondered.

"Rape is an unforgivable crime."

"Olivia, if you would have listened to my teachings and left that heathen husband of yours, none of this would have happened."

"Don't you dare blame my husband. John is a much better man than you could ever be," she said angrily. At that moment Olivia Kincaid reached into her purse, pulled out a gun and shot him six times. After the first three bullets she said, "That is for the three times you raped Vanessa." She shot once more. "That is for the time you raped Sarah." One more shot. "That is for killing my grandchild and this one is for killing Gloria," she said firing the last bullet. She walked towards his body to make sure he was dead, then unemotionally walked back to her car.

Olivia walked into her house and very calmly put her purse on the table, picked up the phone and called the Sheriff. She told him where to find Barker's body. After putting the phone back on the cradle, she walked into the kitchen and sat at the table and wrote two letters then after putting another bullet in the gun she took it to her own head.

When they got home Sarah picked up the phone and called her parents. Again no one answered the phone. It was strange to her that both parents would be out at the same time. They never really went anywhere together.

John Kincaid pulled his car into his driveway and got out. He had noticed the Sheriff's car behind him and wondered what was happening. "What's up Sheriff Johnson? How can I help you? Sarah is okay, isn't she?"

"I'm sure she is, John. I haven't talked to her since she left the hospital. I'm here to talk with Mrs. Kincaid."

"What for?"

"She called our office and told us where to find Barker's body. We found it. Shot through six times."

"How did she know he was dead and where to find the body?"

"That's what we want to find out. Can we come in?"

John opened the door and allowed the Sheriff and his deputy inside.

"Livia? Livia where are you? Sheriff needs to talk to you."

"I'll go up and see if she is in the bedroom." John said heading upstairs. The deputy took it upon himself to look around downstairs. He opened the kitchen door and looked inside and gasped at the sight in front of him. "Sheriff, over here," the deputy called out directing the Sheriff to the kitchen. John heard them and ran downstairs.

"Oh dear! John, don't look in there," the Sheriff said trying to hold John back but John pushed his way passed the Sheriff. "Oh no! Livia." He put his hand over his mouth and hurried towards the bathroom.

Sarah took a nap for a few hours after coming home from the MacAulay's. Her first thought after getting up was to try and get a hold of her parents again. She was feeling a little anxious about not finding one of them at home. The phone rang a number of times before going into the message machine. She hung up. Tyler walked into the room.

"Still not home?"

"They're not. Its kind of bothering me. I don't know why."

"They might be out doing different errands."

Shortly after Sarah got up from her nap, the doorbell rang. She was still feeling a little tired and decided to lie on the couch to rest.

"Who could this be?" Tyler asked, walking to the door. When he opened the door he was surprised to see Mr. Kincaid. Tyler noticed that he looked drained. He knew something was wrong but couldn't think what else could be. John motioned Tyler outside and told him what had happened. Tyler was in shock.

"I know that you and I thought we could take care of him, but my gosh, poor Mrs. Kincaid. Poor Sarah."

"She has to know, but I am not sure how to tell her," John said looking drained.

"Her little body is so fatigued, I don't know if she can take it," Tyler said exhaustedly. "Well maybe between the both of us, we can help her through it."

Sarah was wondering what was going on. She was just about to get up and investigate when Tyler and her father walked into the living room. "Daddy! I'm surprised to see you. Is everything alright?" She noticed that they both looked very serious. She got up from the couch to hug her father. Tyler looked at John and nodded for him to tell Sarah the news.

"Sarah, first of all Barker is dead." Sarah didn't show much emotion, only curiosity. Then she remembered how angry her dad and Mr. Smith felt when they were told what Barker had done to their girls.

"Daddy, tell me neither you nor Vanessa's dad had anything to do with this?" she asked anxiously.

"No, Sarah neither Allen Smith or I had anything to do with it."

"Then who . . . how?"

He took in a deep breath. This was so difficult. He was afraid the words were going to choke in his throat. "The bad news is Sarah, that your momma did it . . ."

"What? Poor Momma. She will be put in prison. I can't believe she would do that," Sarah said interrupting him in complete shock.

"No Sarah, she won't be going to prison." He looked over at Tyler but Tyler just closed his eyes. He was feeling this man's pain. This was hard for him also but he didn't have to be the bearer of the news.

Sarah saw the way the two men looked at each other. "Where is Momma now, daddy?"

John felt a throb come to his throat. He couldn't hold back any longer. He just had to lay it out. "She's dead, darling. She shot herself." Sarah's knees buckled from under her and she was about to hit the floor when Tyler caught her. He carried her back to the couch. John brought her a glass of water. After drinking some of it, she looked at her dad and asked in a very soft shaky voice, "Why did she do that? I mean shoot Barker and then herself?"

"She left us each a letter. Perhaps she will explain in yours," he said handing her an envelope. "She always took good care of us, Sarah. She always cooked great meals and kept a clean house. She was as good as she could be."

Sarah stood for a moment just looking at the envelope in her hand. "I will go into the bedroom and read it alone, if you both don't mind."

"Of course not dear. Go ahead and take your time," said her father. She went into the room and closed the door. She hesitated. "How could she do this?" she asked crying. After a few minutes she dried her cheeks and eyes and opened the envelope and read the letter.

My dear Sarah:

Please forgive me for what I am about to do. I want you to know I have always loved you even though there were times when it didn't seem like I did. I believe I was always afraid for you that something like rape would happen to you like it did to me. I never expected that it would be by the man that I taught you to respect at all times. Please forgive me for bringing him into your life. I made so many wrong judgments about you. I can now say that I am very proud that you took control of your life, got the education you needed to get the job you wanted and have now found such a wonderful young man who brings the happiness that you deserve into your life. Sarah, I was so wrong but I was so blinded. Please forgive me for the unhappy childhood you had. I am glad that you had the courage to turn your life around. You are a lovely young woman. Tyler is so lucky to have you for his wife. I know you will make him a good one and a good mother to his children. I am also glad that you have a good church with proper Christian teaching.

I am sorry that because of my belief in his teachings you were caused pain and humiliation in your young life. I didn't want you to suffer anymore by going through the court system and having some sleazy defense lawyer try to make you look like a bad person. I shot him three times for the number of times he raped Vanessa, once for raping you, once for killing my unborn grandchild and once for killing Gloria. Keep in close touch with your father.

With love always,
Momma

Tyler and John sat in the living room in silence listening to her sobs. There was nothing to say, only to sit and wait. Tyler's heart ached for her knowing she was in the bedroom reading her mother's death letter. He wished she would come out so he could hold her and comfort her. After all the suffering she had gone through, he didn't know how she could handle anymore. A couple of times John put his hands up to his face and Tyler knew he trying to muffle a sob. He too, was trying to be strong for Sarah. Finally, after about twenty minutes the door opened and Sarah emerged. Her eyes were red and swollen. Both John and Tyler stood up. She walked over to her dad and took his hands.

"I'm sorry Daddy."

"We'll get through this, baby girl," he said putting his arms around her. They both cried openly while holding each other. Tyler wanted to put his arms around them both and cry with them but he knew this was a moment for father and daughter.

After a while they sat back down.

"I thought she was changing and pretty soon everything would be normal. She seemed like she had accepted Tyler and my way of life. In fact she said in the letter that she was happy I had Tyler. The lunch she made us the day I was released from the hospital I thought was the beginning of a new start. She was so different that day. She even, with pride, showed me the cake plate that Tyler had given her."

"I think she was admitting that she had been wrong and you were right with the choice you made for your life. She didn't kill herself because she was afraid of going to prison. Without her church, she didn't know how else to live. After you left, the church was her last stronghold. To give almost twenty years or so of her life to find out it was all lies, was just too much for her. She probably felt there was nothing left for her."

"She did confess that she was wrong and she was glad that I had the courage to turn my life around. She said she was pleased with what I had done."

"I'm really glad she left you with those words. Now you know that you did your momma proud."

"Yes. I always wanted to make her proud of me."

CHAPTER 30

There were a lot of people at her funeral, which surprised Sarah. Tyler's whole family came, which Sarah thought was very respectful of them since they had only met Olivia a few times but she had been, after all, their son's mother-in-law. Uncle Andrew and all his family were there, of course. Mr. Shannon was there and Sarah was surprised to see some of the girls from her old school. *Maybe they've just grown up and realized finally how cruel they had been or perhaps this whole scandal could have made them realize how lucky they were not to have been brought up under this man's teachings,* she thought. She nodded her appreciation to them and they nodded back. Most of the church people were there and Vanessa and her family. John's co-workers and some of his clients were also present. It was a good turnout and Sarah was glad that so many people came to pay their last respects to Olivia Kincaid. "Momma probably would be so surprised at this turnout," she whispered to her dad.

"If she could talk to us she would probably say 'they are making too much of a fuss over me' but she really would be loving it. It makes me feel very pleased," he smiled back at her.

Sarah looked across the cemetery and noticed another funeral was taking place. There was nobody paying his or her last respects *there.* Only the pallbearers and the funeral director were in attendance. She decided that the funeral director had probably hired the pallbearers. Nobody in this town had respect for the man being buried. No one would want to carry his coffin. Not only had he lied to them and raped their children, but he even killed two of them. Just yesterday the bodies of two women were found under the floorboards of the room where Sarah and Vanessa had been held prisoners. They were the girls that had been missing since last year. Maybe there were even more in other towns. The police started an investigation into the deaths of other young women from the area over the years.

After the service, people came and shared some nice things about Olivia with Sarah and John Kincaid. Most of them were from the church. John was pleased that they thought so much of her. After most of them were gone, Sarah noticed a man coming towards her. She recognized Martin, Gloria's boyfriend before her death. "I'm sorry, Sarah," Martin said putting his arms around her and giving her a kiss on the cheek."

"Thank you, Martin and thank you for coming."

"I want to thank you Tyler. I heard from your Uncle Dan that you found the girls and helped lead to the capture of Gloria's murderer."

"You're welcome but I only had a part in it."

Martin looked across the graveyard, "Is that him?"

Tyler followed his gaze, "Yes!"

Tyler and Sarah walked up the hill towards the car. Sarah saw a woman standing off a little ways. She knew this was her dad's friend, Kathleen. She nodded to her and the woman nodded back. Sarah thought how respectful of her to come but to keep her distance. Sarah agreed in her heart that she would have her dad and Kathleen over sometime for dinner. Her dad had shared with her that he was looking to move closer to Austin. He would keep his business where it was but would eventually move it to Austin. She knew that in time he and Kathleen would marry. Sarah was happy that her dad and Kathleen would become part of their family gatherings along with the MacAulay's. She was just sad that it couldn't have been that way with her mother.

They drove down Main Street passing the church. "I think the town will tear that place down. It is a reminder of a disgraceful thing that happened here."

"I heard some talk among the men of the congregation that they wanted it burned to the ground as well as the parsonage," Tyler said. "I think the whole town feels humiliated and sick that they had been so vulnerable to this man, who called himself the holy servant of God."

"I can't wait to get out of this place. I am so tired of the way I have been feeling these past months. I want to feel happy again and excited about my life.

"Well now it is all over and we can get back to normal. What would make you happy right now?" asked Tyler.

She looked at him for a while then said, "For us to get on with our lives, our love, our marriage. I want to concentrate on those things

"That's exactly what we are going to do. Later we will plan a honeymoon, but for now I just want to concentrate on making you happy.

"Thank you husband, she said and leaned over and kissed his cheek. "I love and depend on you so much. I know everything will be wonderful." After a few moments she said more solemnly, "It is ironic, darling, that my mother who kept me under her control is the person who eventually set me free. To be honest, I am glad he is dead. I just wish that mom hadn't been the vehicle that killed him."

She sat silent for a few moments more then continued, "I lost a very good friend and my mother all because of that maniac who actually thought he was God. Just when I felt free and happy, he tried to take it away from me, but my momma was the one who ultimately gave me my freedom. She gave up her life for me."

T<small>ATE</small> P<small>UBLISHING</small>, LLC

Tate Publishing is committed to excellence in the publishing industry. Our staff of highly trained professionals—editors, graphic designers, and marketing personnel—work together to produce the very finest book products available. The company reflects in every aspect the philosophy established by the founders based on Psalms 68:11, "The Lord gave the word and great was the company of those who published it."

If you would like further information, please call
1.888.361.9473
or visit our website at
www.tatepublishing.com

Tate Publishing LLC
127 E. Trade Center Terrace
Mustang, Oklahoma 73064 USA